Melanie ON THE MOVE

Like many of us, Melanie finds herself in circumstances where she has difficulty seeing the good. Even so, her new church community is ready to show her and her family the love of Christ. Whether already people of faith or still seeking, readers young and old can join Melanie on her journey as she takes steps closer to the light.

—S. E. M. Ishida,
author of the "Nick Newton" series

Carefully weaving the events of *Melanie On The Move,* author J.D. Rempel compels the reader to search for "an understanding of the truth behind the fiction." The title character, caught up in a series of seemingly unfair circumstances, is drawn to examine her view of the world when she's challenged by the message of Romans 8:28 ("God works all things for the good to those who love him").

—Susan Bollinger,
Teacher/Literacy Coach

Melanie ON THE MOVE

The NorCal Girls
BOOK ONE

J.D. REMPEL

AMBASSADOR INTERNATIONAL
GREENVILLE, SOUTH CAROLINA & BELFAST, NORTHERN IRELAND
www.ambassador-international.com

Melanie on the Move

The NorCal Girls, Book 1

ISBN: 978-1-62020-953-0
eISBN: 978-1-62020-965-3

Library of Congress Control Number: 2020935268

Cover Design and Page Layout by Hannah Nichols
eBook Conversion by Anna Riebe Raats
Edited by Daphne Self

AMBASSADOR INTERNATIONAL
Emerald House
411 University Ridge, Suite B14
Greenville, SC 29601, USA
www.ambassador-international.com

AMBASSADOR BOOKS
The Mount
2 Woodstock Link
Belfast, BT6 8DD, Northern Ireland, UK
www.ambassadormedia.co.uk

The colophon is a trademark of Ambassador, a Christian publishing company.

For my family,

Poppy, Mommy, and Sissy,

and the memories we share of our vacations

driving in the ranchero to family camp

to Alliance Redwoods.

Love you Xoxoxinfinity!!!

1

NORMAL LIFE

Melanie Cooper huddled under her blankets with a flashlight, reading a mystery. Her eyes would barely stay open, but she wanted to finish just one more chapter. If she stayed up much longer, she'd be too tired for her swim meet tomorrow. As she turned the page, Melanie heard footsteps in the hallway. Immediately, she clicked off her flashlight and shoved the evidence of her late-night routine beneath her pillow.

"I wish we'd been able to sell the cabin instead." Dad's voice penetrated through Melanie's closed door.

"Shush, you're going to wake the girls, Jack." Mom tried to whisper.

"It could have solved most of our problems."

"We'll make it work, somehow. But we need to tell the girls soon."

Her parents' voices trailed off.

What did they need to tell them? What was going on? The cabin—they hadn't been there in years. But why would they need to sell it? Her stomach knotted. It always did when she was scared. Katie had told her if she was ever scared, she could pray and ask God to help her. Why did that thought pop into her head? Maybe her best friend's religion was rubbing off on her. She shook her head and pushed the idea aside. She didn't need God. Mom and Dad would take care of everything. Wouldn't they?

***

Melanie stood near her swim lane. Before the heat, she shook out her arms, shrugged her shoulders, and bounced on her feet to release her nervous energy and loosen up her muscles. She checked her swim cap to make sure all her hair was secured, then adjusted her goggles. When the starter announced for the swimmers to take their marks, Melanie climbed onto the block and leaned into her stance. The signal sounded and she dove into the water.

Pull, breathe, kick, glide. Pull, breathe, kick, glide. It was the steps of the breaststroke and it was

Melanie's mantra as she swam. She touched the wall and pushed off to complete her lap. Pull, breathe, kick, glide. In under a minute, she palmed the pool wall with both hands.

She grabbed the edge and kicked her legs, trying to catch her breath while she waited for the rest of the swimmers to finish. Climbing out of the pool, Melanie glanced with anticipation at the score board for her race time. Her heart pounded as it lit up. She was in first place and had beaten her personal best, trimming off a couple hundredths of a second. She squealed and gave a high-five to her teammate, Torie.

Melanie turned toward the bleachers and scanned the crowd for her parents. They waved and cheered. She was so relieved Dad was able to make it today. Things had changed so much since he'd lost his job. Now that he spent most of his time doing contracting work with different business firms, he no longer had time to help coach her in swimming and rarely attended her meets.

Is that what her parents had been whispering about last night? Was her dad's consultant business failing? Or was it about her school? Maybe she would have to leave Lynnwood Academy. Her sister, Megan, would hate that and so would she.

Melanie sighed and shook her head. No, no distractions; she needed to concentrate. Her next race was coming up and her teammates were counting on her.

Her second event was the team medley relay. Melanie hovered in position over the water waiting for her teammate's fingertips to touch the wall. When they did, Melanie dove in and coursed through the water for her lap. As her hand contacted the wall, Cassidy sprang over her. Melanie quickly pulled herself out of the pool and moved aside to cheer on her team.

After the meet, Melanie and Torie collected their ribbons at the award's table.

"Mel, have you finished your project for history yet?"

"Almost."

Torie sighed. "I'm halfway done, but I have to work on it this afternoon. Ugh!"

Melanie laughed. "It's not that bad."

"Well, I'm sure it's no big deal when you're the teacher's pet."

Melanie elbowed her. "Am not. Mr. Carlisle doesn't have any favorites. He just appreciates my enthusiasm."

"Yeah, enthusiasm for dry, old history. Boring." She rolled her eyes. "Hey, we're going out for pizza like usual for lunch. Want to come?"

"Sure. I'll just have to ask my parents."

Dad planted his hand on Melanie's shoulder. "Ask your parents what?"

"Mr. Cooper, I invited Melanie to go out to pizza with my family. Of course, you and Mrs. Cooper can come, too, if you'd like."

He smiled politely. "No, we can't today. Thanks for the offer."

Torie shrugged.

"Great job today, girls."

Melanie scrunched up her features. "I wish we'd done better on the medley."

"Your team got second, and your team ranked third overall."

"Not good enough."

"Did you do your best?"

"Of course, I did."

"Did your team do their best?"

"Of course."

Torie nodded in agreement.

"Then it is good enough."

Melanie smiled. "Then, if we were good enough. Maybe I should be rewarded with pizza. Pleeeeeease."

He frowned. "Mel, not this time."

"Pretty please, Daddy."

He flushed. "Melanie, I said, no!"

Torie raised her eyebrows and pursed her lips. "Okay then, I better get going. I'll see you in class on Monday, Mel. Or I might call you if I need help with my assignment."

Melanie nodded as she tried to hold back the tears threatening to fall.

Torie backed away. "Bye, Mel. Bye, Mr. Cooper."

"Bye, Torie," Dad said as Melanie waved.

Melanie remained silent as they walked quickly to the car. She took deep breaths so she wouldn't cry, but one tear escaped. What was going on? Why had Dad said no? It wasn't like it was the first time Torie had ever asked her to go out for pizza after a swim meet. And why had he gotten so upset about it?

Had she done something? No, it had to be that secret her parents were keeping from her and Megan. Melanie bit her lip. She should ask them about it. But then she'd have to confess that she'd been reading late and eavesdropping. Dad was already mad, and she didn't want to make it worse. What could she do? She groaned. Nothing. Absolutely nothing.

2

THE DECISION

After a restless night's sleep, Melanie woke to the smell of frying bacon. She stretched her arms over her head and flexed her shoulders. Bounding out of bed, she grabbed a barrette from the nightstand and clipped back her long, brown hair.

When she entered the kitchen, Dad was seated at the table, reading the newspaper. Over the pages, he playfully glared at her through his glasses. "How late did you read last night? It's not like our mermaid to miss a morning swim."

She bit her lip and lowered her eyes. She hadn't been reading, but Melanie did not want him to know why she hadn't slept well. And she certainly didn't want him to know what she'd overheard the other night.

"That's what I thought." He shook his head. "Maybe I should take away that flashlight."

"Ah, Dad, but why can't I read at night? It's the weekend. And I'm almost a teenager."

"Don't remind me." He grunted. "But if I ever catch you on a school night . . . "

"I know." She kissed him on the cheek.

Scooting into her chair, she watched as her mom brought over a platter of steaming chocolate-chip pancakes. Melanie forked two fluffy pancakes onto her plate, and then she slathered them with butter and syrup.

Her older sister, dressed in her pink pajamas, shuffled in half asleep. Megan flopped down into her chair. Even with her hair tousled and her blue eyes filled with sleep, she was beautiful. She looked exactly like their mother.

After Mom poured herself a cup of coffee and joined them, Dad set aside his newspaper. "We have something very important we need to tell you girls."

Melanie's stomach churned as she remembered the conversation she had overheard the other night. Her fork fell clattering onto her plate.

Dad cleared his throat. "Money has been tight since I was laid off last year. So your mother and I have made a decision." He smiled weakly and took a deep breath. "We're selling the house. We have decided to live up at the cabin."

"What?" Megan spurted out. The orange juice she'd been drinking dribbled down her chin. She wiped her face with a napkin. "But you have a job."

"Yes, but it's only temporary and it will be ending soon. We cannot afford to live here anymore." His lips tightened.

"This doesn't make sense." Megan rolled her eyes. "I don't believe it."

But Melanie knew it was true.

Megan lifted her chin. "Oh, I know. Just borrow the money from Grandma and Grandpa."

Dad's face reddened. "I will not ask for money from my parents. This family is my responsibility!"

"But it's not fair!"

Mom glowered at Megan. "Megan, that's enough."

"Well, you can't do this to me! I'm not going!" Megan's chair flew back as she stood. "I'll stay with one of my friends! I'll never live in that filthy, old cabin." She stormed out of the kitchen, stomped up the stairs, and slammed her bedroom door.

Melanie swallowed hard. "When will we move?"

"As soon as school ends," Mom answered.

Melanie couldn't stop the tears and her voice cracked when she spoke. "But what about Katie? We've been best friends since kindergarten. What am I going to tell her? And what about my swimming? Does this mean I have to quit the swim team? And, now I won't have my pool to practice in anymore. What about my birthday? I always have a swim party. And, and, and . . . "

Mom came beside her, and Melanie dove into her embrace.

Dad leaned over and stroked her back. "Mel, Mom and I are trying to make this transition as easy for you and Megan as we can. I've already checked the hours for the local pool. We won't be able to go every day, but we'll make sure you get enough practice time. And Megan needs time to adjust to the idea. She can't stay upset with us for too long if she still wants to go on her trip with Ainsley."

Melanie wiped her eyes. "But why did this have to happen to us?"

Her parents had no answer.

***

In the afternoon, Melanie practiced her breaststroke in her pool. When Katie arrived, Melanie swam to the ladder and climbed out. She retrieved her towel, then slumped down next to Katie.

"Mel, what's wrong?" Katie asked as she put her arm around Melanie.

She choked out, "At the end of the school year, we're moving."

"You can't be serious." Katie's eyes teared. "Where?"

"Near Santa Rosa."

Katie elbowed her and gave a relieved gasp. "You scared me. I thought you were moving across the country and I'd never see you again. But moving to the North Bay isn't too far, only about a two-and-a-half-hour drive. I know the area pretty well."

"You do?"

"Yeah, the camp I always go to is up there. So, what town is it?"

"We have a cabin in a place called Occidental."

Katie burst out laughing. "This is incredible."

"What's so funny?" Melanie asked. How could Katie act like this? Didn't she realize how serious this was?

When Katie calmed down, she said, "I'm sorry. It's just that I've hounded you to go to camp with me, and now I find out you had a cabin there all along. It's . . . well, it's ironic." Katie nudged her. "Now maybe you'll finally go to camp with me."

"I guess." How could Melanie explain she still wasn't interested in going to Katie's church camp without hurting her feelings?

"Think of all the things you can do: exploring, hiking, canoeing. It would be so cool to live that close to the Russian River. You can go canoeing all the time." Katie smiled. "I'm a little jealous."

Melanie snorted. "Then maybe you should move there and leave the only life you've ever known. How can you be so happy about this?"

Katie's eyes grew big and she sputtered out. "Of course, I'm not happy about it, it's just . . . the times I've been there mean so much to me that I can't imagine being unhappy there." She drew her shoulders back. "And I have . . . well . . . I just know God will take care of you."

Melanie frowned and stood up. "So God wants me unhappy? He wants to take away the things I love—my friends and my pool. I should have known you would put a religious spin on this." She ran into the house. If even her best friend didn't understand her, who would?

3

CHANGES

Melanie dragged herself out of their overloaded SUV. Dad drove up in his car and parked beside them on the driveway. Tall redwood trees loomed over the A-frame cabin with its aged, red siding. She breathed in the woodsy-scented air. But instead of the dread she'd felt on the way, peace enveloped her.

Mom pulled open the creaky screen and unlocked the worn front door. Melanie followed her parents inside. The room and its old-fashioned furniture were familiar to her, like an old friend she hadn't visited in a while. Memories of the times spent at the cabin flooded her: sitting on the hearth roasting marshmallows in the fireplace, reading in the loft with the sunlight filtering through the skylights, swaying on the porch swing, and watching water skitters dance on the water.

The creek! How could she have forgotten about that? Was it real or just a dream? She raced down the hallway toward the back door.

Her mom called out, "Melanie, where are you going?"

"To the creek, Mom, to the creek!"

She heard Mom chuckle. "Just for a little while. We need your help to unload."

"Sure thing."

At the back door, Melanie took a quick peek into the room she would be sharing with Megan. She would have it all to herself for the summer since Megan was in Hawaii with her friend, Ainsley and her family.

Melanie's palm was sweaty as she tried to unlock the door. The lock finally gave and she rushed outside. Melanie leapt out onto the porch and bounded down the steps. She took the dusty path down to the water's edge. It was just as she remembered it. Even a lone water skitter darted across the water's surface. Melanie bit her lip. Maybe it wouldn't be so bad living here after all.

***

After what seemed like hours and hours of unpacking, Melanie's stomach rumbled loudly. How much longer would they be working? It had seemed like forever since they'd had lunch.

Dad entered her room. "Get your sweatshirt."

"Dinner. Finally."

He laughed. "I guess we've worked you pretty hard today."

Melanic grabbed her sweatshirt, passed Dad, and headed for the front door.

"Wrong way, Mel."

"What?" She turned. It was then she noticed he was standing at the back door with a flashlight in his hand, even though it was still light outside. "Where are we going?"

Mom came up behind her. "Vivian invited us over."

"Who's Vivian?"

"She's our next-door neighbor."

They went out the back and trekked along the dirt path. It wound around, up and down, and up again. The creek meandered through a steep gully on one side and on the other was a jumble of bushes with clusters of tall trees. At a partial clearing, a set of wooden stairs led up to the second story of a white-planked house. At the top deck, Dad knocked on the door.

An older woman wearing a stylish emerald-green shorts outfit answered. Her shoulder-length gray hair was pulled back elegantly away from her face. She seemed familiar.

"Vivian," Dad roared, hugging the lady. Mom came up and squeezed her, too.

"Come in, come in," Vivian said.

Mom laid a hand on Melanie's shoulder. "Vivian, you remember our younger daughter, Melanie?"

"Oh, yes. Hello sweetheart." Vivian exclaimed. "I don't think I've seen you since . . . " Her eyes misted and she wiped away the tears. "How long has it actually been?"

"About seven years." Mom turned to Melanie. "Melanie, you remember our neighbor, Vivian?"

From the smile Vivian gave her, Melanie knew they would be friends. Melanie grinned and clasped Vivian's hand warmly.

Vivian led them through her living room. The adults talked while Melanie checked out her surroundings. The most dominant feature of the room was a grand piano nestled into the alcove of a large bay window. A formal floral couch and loveseat were flanked by ornate end tables. Framed opera posters hung on the walls.

They followed Vivian into the dining room where the huge table was loaded with food. There was green salad, dinner rolls, roasted vegetables, pasta salad, and centered in the middle was a steaming dish of lasagna, Melanie's favorite. Her mouth watered.

During dinner she occasionally heard a chorus of chirping and squawking coming from behind her. Puzzled, she turned around and saw French doors. "There sure are some noisy birds around here," Melanie commented.

Vivian laughed. "That ruckus is coming from my aviary."

"Really? That's cool. How many birds do you have?"

"I haven't counted them lately but I'd say . . . " She paused whispering to herself and counting on her fingers. "Oh, I'm not sure—probably somewhere in the neighborhood of twenty."

"Wow. Can we see them?"

Dad gave her a warning look. "Not right now, Mel."

Vivian agreed. "Yes, it will be too dark in there after dinner. Why don't you come over Wednesday about three o'clock to see them?"

Melanie shrugged, "Okay." Four days. Why couldn't she come tomorrow or the next day? It was kind of strange. Why would Vivian make her wait so long?

***

On Sunday afternoon, as Melanie continued to unpack, she heard her parents arguing in their room. What was wrong now? She snuck down the hallway and stood outside their bedroom door. Drawers opened and then slammed shut. What was going on? Were they leaving?

"Jack, you said you would look for a job here."

"I already gave my word, Gretchen. Besides, we really don't have a choice."

"But where will you stay?"

"One of the men offered me his guest room. I'll come back on the weekends."

"But we agreed to make the cabin our home."

"If it was up to me, we wouldn't have moved at all. But circumstances weren't in our favor. I have a feeling this job will become permanent, and when it does, I'll find us an apartment. This could be the break we need to get back on track." His voice sounded hopeful.

Melanie's heart hammered and her stomach quivered. What did he mean? Dad wouldn't be living with them? Why couldn't they stay together? This move was tearing her family apart.

"Jack, you already know how I feel. I believe we could make a good life up here. I thought this would be a new start for all of us."

He cleared his throat. "I need to get going before traffic gets too heavy."

When he exited the bedroom, Melanie wrapped her arms around his waist. "Daddy, I don't want you to go."

He leaned over and kissed the top of her head. "I know, but we need the money. Your mom will explain." He released her and pulled his suitcase behind him. Melanie trailed him outside.

Dad put his bag in the trunk, and then slammed it shut.

"Why can't we go with you?"

"Mel, you can't. It's complicated."

"Daddy, please."

"That's enough!" He shook his head and sighed. "I'm sorry. I'll be back next weekend, and I promise I'll take you swimming." He got into his car and sped away before she could reply.

4

NEW FRIENDS

As Melanie climbed up Vivian's back steps, she heard a strong soprano voice accompanied by a piano. Whoever was singing had a lovely voice. Melanie waited on the landing, not wanting to interrupt. The melody was light and fanciful, giving Melanie the sense of what a summer day would sound like, if it were set to music. When the song ended, Melanie knocked.

"You're right on time." Vivian opened the screen door and escorted Melanie inside.

On the other side of the piano, a girl Melanie's age gathered up sheet music. She had long, light-brown hair and blue eyes. The girl gave Melanie a huge smile and stepped around the bench. "Hi, I'm Cindy. You must be Melanie. Vivian has told me tons about you. She told me you're from Silicon Valley and you have an older sister. I'm stuck in the middle of two brothers. I think I would rather have a sister."

Smiling, Melanie opened her mouth to respond, but she couldn't get a word in.

"Vivian said you're twelve." Cindy took a breath.

"Actually, I'll be thirteen in a couple of weeks."

Cindy squealed. "I will be thirteen in August. So, what kinds of things do you like to do? Oh, wait, that's right, I heard you like to swim. You should meet JB. He is a really good swimmer and has won some trophies."

Melanie grinned proudly. "I've won a few, too. My best event is the breaststroke."

"Cool. I'd love to see you swim. We should go swimming sometime."

"I'd like that."

"Hey, I have God's Rock tonight. You should come. It's loads of fun."

"God's what?"

"God's Rock, it's the name of our youth group. Sorry, I know I talk way too much and way too fast. My family teases me all the time about it, especially my brothers, Trevor and Tyler."

Melanie giggled. "I don't mind. My family says the opposite about me, except when I'm talking about swimming."

A car honked from the driveway.

"That's them." Cindy looked at her watch, and then shoved her music into a folder. "They're here early. I was hoping we would have more time to get to know each other. But we'll have time for that tonight at God's Rock."

"Well, I'm not . . . "

"So, I'll see you tonight. It starts at six thirty." The horn blared, louder and longer. "Brothers." Cindy huffed, rolling her eyes. "Bye." She raced out the front door, letting it slam behind her.

Vivian chuckled and shook her head. "Cindy is a whirlwind."

"So, was she here for a voice lesson?" Melanie asked.

"Yes. I started giving voice lessons a few years ago. Before that I was a professional singer."

"An opera singer, right? I saw your posters."

"Yes, that's very observant of you." She smiled. "Now, it seems I remember promising you a chance to see my birds." Vivian led her to the French doors. When she opened them, Melanie followed and stepped into an enormous, circular glass bird house.

The glass structure was filled with lush plants, trees, and flowers. Water gurgled from a waterfall into a small pond. Birds chirped as they flew from branch to branch.

Wings spread wide, a bird dove toward her. Melanie closed her eyes and ducked. What was the bird going to do? She felt the weight of the bird as it landed on her back. Melanie straightened. The bird's claws poked through her t-shirt as it climbed up, finally resting on her shoulder. Opening her eyes, she turned her head and glimpsed a bright green bird.

"Paco." Vivian gasped in astonishment.

Melanie's voice shook. "Will he bite me? He has a really big beak."

Paco moved closer and nibbled on her hair. Melanie squealed.

"It's all right. He isn't trying to bite you," Vivian assured her. "He is actually preening you, which is so sweet."

"What?"

"Preening is when birds clean and take care of their feathers. Birds will preen other birds who are their mates. Paco is helping you with your 'feathers.' I've never seen him act like this before. He really likes you."

"What kind of bird is he?"

"He is a grey-cheeked parakeet," Vivian answered.

"But he looks too big to be a parakeet."

"Yes, grey-cheeks are bigger than budgies, which are the kind of parakeets you usually see at the pet store."

Vivian stretched out her arm. A large red-and blue-parrot flew to her. "And this is Sheba. The Queen of Sheba, actually." Vivian pulled out some bird seed from her pocket. Paco leapt off Melanie's shoulder and landed on Vivian. Some of the other birds came, too, and ate right out of Vivian's hand.

"How do you like living here?"

Melanie shrugged. "It's not too bad, I guess." She was quiet for a time. "I miss my dad and my friends, and I guess I miss Megan, too, even if she's really bossy."

"Older sisters are like that." Vivian chuckled and asked, "Why do you miss your dad? I thought he'd moved up here, too."

"That was the plan, but he got a job."

"That's wonderful news." Vivian said.

"It's all right, but we can't live with him, at least for now."

"How long will you be staying?"

Melanie wrinkled her forehead and pursed her lips. "I really don't know. Everything is kind of up in the air.

Mom wants us to live here, but Dad wants to move back if we can." It was all so confusing. She really didn't want to think about it right now.

Vivian pulled out a bag of sliced fruit. Would you like to give them a treat?"

"Um. I'm not sure. I haven't been around birds like this before."

Vivian smiled reassuringly. "They are very friendly. All of them have been hand-fed since they were babies, so they are familiar with people."

"I don't know."

"Just give it a try."

"Okay." Melanie walked over and grabbed a few pieces.

Melanie opened her hand with her palm facing upward. Paco chirped, flew back over to her, and began eating. The other birds seemed content being with Vivian.

Vivian's eyes sparkled with amusement. "He's really taken with you. If you like, you can come over and play with him whenever you like."

Melanie bit her lip and nodded.

Vivian continued, "I overheard Cindy invite you to God's Rock tonight. It meets at our church. My women's Bible study is held there at the same time. If you want to go, I can take you."

“I’ll think about it.” Oh, why did she have to say that? The last thing she wanted to do was go to church and have anything to do with God, especially after all the things her family had been going through.

5

GOD'S ROCK

Melanie walked through the church building and followed the loud music to where the youth would be meeting. She hadn't had a choice about going to God's Rock. Her mom had decided for her when Vivian had invited her mom to women's Bible study. But why had she insisted on coming in alone? Was Cindy even there yet? How was she going to find her? Melanie bit her lip and her stomach started to hurt.

"Melanie," Cindy called out, running toward her from the other end of the hallway. When she reached Melanie, Cindy hooked her arm through Melanie's. "I knew you'd come. I'm so glad you're here early so I can give you the tour." They reached double doors and turned into a wider hallway which had multiple doors on either side.

Cindy waved her hand to the left. "Those are the youth pastors' offices." Music blared from the next room and Cindy explained, "That's our youth room, which I'll show you last." They hurried past the restrooms and a kitchenette. The hallway led them to the gymnasium where a group of boys played basketball.

"Over here! Over here!" A man with crazy spiked brown hair waved his arms to his teammates. One of the players passed him the ball, but he missed, and the ball rolled to Melanie. She scooped it up and threw it back to the guy. He gave her a sweeping bow. "Thank you, fair lady."

She laughed. What a goof.

Cindy pointed and continued with her description. "On the other side of the gym are more bathrooms, and the high school youth room. I'd show it to you, but they keep it locked because the high schoolers don't like us *children* going in there." Cindy rolled her eyes. "Anyway, on to the game room."

They entered the door opposite the kitchenette. Inside the massive room were two ping-pong tables, an air hockey table, a pool table, a foosball table, and a few arcade games. The place was packed. It was such a cool hangout, not like any church Melanie had ever seen.

At the foosball table, a boy with blond hair looked up at her and gave her a lopsided grin. Her heart thumped wildly, and she blushed. He was so cute!

Cindy pulled her away. "All right. Last stop, I want to introduce you to the gang."

In the youth room, couches formed a U-shape around a small platform at the front, creating a wide open area. Cindy and Melanie reached the back couch. A girl sitting there smiled up at them.

An Asian girl with short black hair, who was sprawled across a gigantic bean bag chair, teased Cindy. "Wow, Cin, I can't believe you're here on time."

Cindy smirked at the girl. "If you must know, Trevor came early to practice, and I wanted to be here when Melanie arrived. So, guys, this is Melanie, the one I told you about."

"I'm Rachel." The girl on the couch said, offering Melanie a seat. Rachel had shoulder-length brown hair and a sunny smile.

Cindy interjected, "And the sarcastic one is Haley."

"Hey, that's not nice," Haley objected.

"All right. Sorry. Haley is the jokester of our group."

Haley nodded. "Hmm. That sounds about right."

Cindy looked around. "Where's Ella?"

Haley guffawed. "Ella is always late on Wednesday nights. She has softball practice, but I guess you wouldn't know since you always get here after she does."

Cindy stuck her tongue out at Haley.

The music stopped. Those already in the room became quiet, and the others came in and took seats on the other couches or the floor.

The goofy guy with the spiked hair bounded on stage. "Hey, guys."

The group responded in unison, "Hey, Pastor Brett."

No way! He was the youth pastor? She couldn't believe it and would've never guessed this man was a pastor.

His voice boomed out. "I know there are some new faces." He raised his eyebrows and locked Melanie in his gaze. "But I won't embarrass you by making you stand up and introduce yourselves. We just wanted to let you know we're glad you're here. So, welcome." Cindy nudged her, and Melanie breathed a sigh of relief.

"Our only announcement is to remind you about the camp fundraiser. If you want to sign up for it, please talk to Bonnie. Can I see a show of hands again of who's going to camp?" An army of hands raised. "Great. Then we should have quite a few volunteers for the fundraiser."

Wow! So many of them were going to camp. Wouldn't that be funny if it was the same camp Katie went to?

When Pastor Brett finished, a young guy with shaggy blond hair, which hung in his eyes, stepped onto the platform carrying a guitar. He sat down onto a stool and began to play. The lights dimmed, and words to the music flashed on the wall behind him. A girl wearing a baseball cap with her hair in a ponytail came in and sat next to Cindy.

Leaning over, Cindy whispered, "This is Ella and the guy playing the guitar is my brother, Trevor."

The kids stood, sang, and clapped. Melanie remained seated and bit her lip. This singing stuff was kind of weird. Cindy nudged Melanie's leg and smiled down at her while she sang. Her sweet voice was louder than the others. After the singing, Pastor Brett came back on stage.

Oh great, a sermon. How long was this going to take? Melanie didn't want to hear about God. She tuned out Pastor Brett and decided it would be a good opportunity to look for the cute boy. From her vantage point, she skimmed the crowd. But she couldn't find him. He must be here somewhere. Searching again, she caught a glimpse of blond, but her view was blocked.

"God loves us and only wants the best for us," Pastor Brett emphasized.

What? She looked up.

"That doesn't mean life is going to be perfect or easy. Most likely it won't be. Yes, you heard me right. Most likely our lives will be filled with difficulties and disappointments. But there's hope. God can use it for good like it says in Romans 8:28. Does anyone have that verse memorized? Or maybe someone can read it out loud?"

A guy spoke up, "And we know that God causes all things to work together for good to those who love God, to those who are called according to His purpose."

"Thank you, JB. Does this mean once you become a Christian everything will be perfect?"

There were murmurs of no.

He shook his head. "No, it doesn't. But I do believe God uses your circumstances to pull you closer to Him. If you do believe, He uses them to make you more like Him. If you don't believe, He's trying to draw you closer into knowing Him."

Melanie already believed God existed. But why would she want to know God better when He had made things more difficult for her? It didn't make any sense. True, she had only gone to Katie's church once or twice in the many years they'd been friends. She'd lived here less than a week, and she was already at youth group. Was God using this move to draw her closer to Him? Maybe there was something to all this God stuff after all. She knew Katie believed it and it seemed like everyone else here did, too.

"Amen," the crowd said. She hadn't noticed they'd been praying.

Afterwards, the girls gathered around her, hounding her with questions about her life. It was overwhelming in the beginning, but the more they chatted, the more comfortable she felt.

"Hope to see you Sunday, Melanie," Haley said. She tilted her head. "Or should I call you mermaid?" She grinned, wiggling her eyebrows.

"Sure. It's what my dad calls me."

One by one the girls left, so Melanie decided to wait by the double doors for her mom and Vivian. A bulletin board hung on the wall displaying photos of the youth group. She saw pictures of Cindy, Rachel, Haley, Ella, and the boy with the blond hair. In the photos they were ice skating, handing out food boxes, at concerts, and participating in other activities.

Another section had the word CAMP over it and had a collage of candid snapshots of smiling kids hiking along trails, sitting around a campfire, playing volleyball, and canoeing. Beside the collage, a plastic box held colorful camp brochures. She selected one of the glossy pamphlets and read through it. Maybe she did want to go to camp.

"Mel, are you ready to go?" Her mother's voice startled her.

Melanie quickly stuffed the camp brochure into her pocket.

6

ADJUSTMENTS

"Mom, I'm bored." Melanie leaned against the white tiled kitchen counter as Mom washed the dinner dishes.

"You could help dry."

Melanie rolled her eyes and made an over-exaggerated huff. "I guess." But she really didn't mind and she grabbed a dish towel.

"Vivian invited us to go to church with her on Sunday."

"Yeah, she already asked me, but I told her I couldn't go since Dad will be home." Melanie paused. "But even if I could, I wouldn't want to go."

Mom handed her a dish. "Why not? Didn't you have a fun time at youth group?"

Melanie nodded. "I really like the kids there. But it isn't about youth group."

Mom turned off the water. "Then, what is this about?"

Melanie shrugged.

"We're not leaving this kitchen until you tell me what's bothering you." Her voice held concern.

Melanie confessed, "It's about God."

"What about God?"

"I just . . . I just don't really like Him right now."

"Why?"

"Because of all the bad things which have happened to us."

Mom shook her head. "But what about the good things? Your dad found another job. We were able to sell our house, which is nearly impossible in this market. And"—she smiled—"the best part for me has been the extra time I've been able to spend with you."

"But Dad's not here, and I can't go swimming every day."

"Mel, life is never going to be perfect, but we have so much to be thankful for." She tapped the tip of Melanie's nose with bubbles from the dishwashing soap. "You never know. Maybe church would be good for us."

Melanie wiped off the suds. "So when do you think Dad will be home? I thought he would be here by now."

"He should be home any minute. Traffic is always horrible on Fridays."

The phone rang and Mom picked it up. "Hey, we were just talking about you." Cradling the phone on her shoulder, she dried her hands. She paused, listening. "Oh, Jack you can't . . . " Mom's voice trembled. "Yes, we'll talk about it later." Mom put the phone back on the receiver slowly.

Melanie bit her lip. "Well?"

Mom turned to her. "Your dad has a pile of work to do. He won't be coming home this weekend. I'm sorry, sweetheart. I know how much you were looking forward to it."

Melanie swallowed hard, trying to keep from crying. Her voice shook. "But he promised to take me swimming, and he's never broken a promise to me before."

"I can take you, if you'd like."

"Okay." Melanie sniffed. But why did Dad have to break his promise? No, it wasn't Dad's fault. He was just trying to provide for his family. God allowed this to happen even though she'd been going to church. So no more church. It didn't matter if she was making new friends. She was never going there again!

***

Melanie skimmed the mystery section of the library. She wished she could check out an armload of books, but Mom was limiting her to three. Two of them were nestled on her arm. It was different getting books at the library; usually Mom took her to the bookstore and bought her whatever she wanted. But they couldn't afford that anymore.

Engrossed in her search, Melanie hardly noticed someone else in the aisle with her. The person came up alongside her and gently elbowed her.

Melanie turned and let out a surprised gasp. It was Cindy.

Cindy chuckled softly. "I was thinking about putting my hands over your eyes and saying 'Guess who' but I thought you might scream. And we wouldn't want that, especially here." She giggled. "I can't believe I ran into you today."

"Actually, you bumped into me." Melanie elbowed Cindy back.

"Ha, ha." Cindy scoffed. "Anyway, I was hoping we could hang out, but I didn't have your phone number."

Melanie confessed reluctantly, "I don't have my own phone, just a home phone."

"Me, too," Cindy said.

"Really? I thought I was the only one. My parents said I have to wait until I'm in high school."

"If I want one, I have to pay for it myself. I'd rather use my allowance and babysitting money on something else, like helping my parents with my camp costs." Cindy glanced at the books Melanie carried. "What did you get?"

"Just mysteries. They're my favorite. How about you?"

"I like mysteries, too, but I adore sci-fi and fantasy."

"I haven't read any of those kind."

"No way. You'll love them. Come on, I'll pick out some good ones for you." Cindy pulled her into the fantasy section.

"My mom said I can only have one more book."

Cindy groaned. "Then, it's really going to be too hard to choose. Hmm." She put her finger to her lips. "Oh, I've got it." She went to another row and squatted down. "Here it is." She tugged out a book. "It's one of my favorites." Cindy handed it to Melanie. "Now, I need to find something for me. What should I get?"

"Nope, it's my turn." Melanie grabbed Cindy and headed back to the mysteries. Locating some of her favorites, Melanie dug out one book after another, and handed them off to Cindy. "Have you read this?" Every time Cindy responded in the negative, Melanie put another book into her arms.

"I think this is more than I can read in a week." Cindy exclaimed. "But this is fun. None of my other friends like to read as much as I do. It's nice to have a friend I can discuss books with, and who will want to go to the library with me."

"My best friend Katie loves to read, too. I'm glad to have another friend who shares my love of books." She smiled.

The girls headed to the front. They placed their selections on the front counter and waited as the librarian scanned their library cards and books. When she had finished, they hauled their treasures toward the exit. Mom was waiting for her, but she was talking with another lady who looked a bit like Cindy.

"Is that your mom?" Melanie inquired.

"Yep. Your mom told me you were here. Our moms know each other from Bible study."

Introductions were made. The girls exchanged phone numbers. Then it was time to leave.

Cindy said, “I’ll see you tomorrow.”

Melanie gave her a puzzled look.

“At church.” She smiled and walked out the door.

Church. Melanie groaned.

7

SUNDAY SCHOOL

Melanie wasn't happy about it, but she went along with Mom to church. She was determined to ignore anything anyone said about God. She was only going to get to know her friends better and maybe find out more about camp. If Cindy was willing to use her own money to go, it must be really fun. And maybe she could find out the name of the cute boy. The morning might not be a total waste.

Since Vivian knew the way, she walked with Melanie down the hallway to her Sunday school classroom. Melanie's stomach knotted and she chewed on her lip.

Vivian gave her a reassuring pat. "Don't worry. Cindy is in your class. And I know you will like your teacher."

Together they entered the room. A lady who looked barely out of high school with short, curly brown hair, fair skin, and freckles sat at a table talking with a group of girls. She had a welcoming smile, and she stood up when she noticed them.

"Hi, Bonnie," Vivian greeted the lady. "This is my neighbor, Melanie." She turned to Melanie. "And Melanie, this is Bonnie. She'll be your teacher."

"Welcome, Melanie," Bonnie said cheerfully.

"Hi," Melanie mumbled and kept her eyes down.

Vivian squeezed Melanie's shoulder and left.

Melanie moved to the table and flopped down into a vacant seat.

"Melanie, that's a fine way to greet your friends," growled a sarcastic voice.

She glanced up into the face of Haley who wiggled her eyebrows at her. And seated next to Haley was a grinning Ella.

"Oh, sorry. I didn't see you."

"Well, that's obvious." Haley snickered.

Bonnie introduced the rest of the girls in the class, then she said, "Let's start our time with prayer."

Melanie frowned and then bowed her head, but she didn't close her eyes. Why wasn't Cindy here? The empty chair next to Melanie quietly slid back and someone sat down. Melanie glanced over. It was Cindy.

For the lesson, Bonnie gave each of them verses to look up in their Bibles.

Melanie fidgeted in her chair. She didn't have a Bible.

Cindy whispered to her. "I can grab you a Bible to use or we can share."

"I think I'd rather share."

Cindy flipped to the right pages quickly. After reading them, Melanie couldn't believe it. The verses were about God drawing people closer to Him. Not this again. Couldn't they find something else to talk about from the Bible? Melanie tried not to listen, but it was hard not to.

When Sunday school was over, Cindy and her friends surrounded Melanie.

"Well, mermaid, did you go swimming this week?" Haley teased.

"No."

Bonnie came up behind them. "Sorry to interrupt, but are any of you volunteering for the fundraiser?" Most of the girls nodded. "Okay, I'll put you guys on the list. Did Brett announce it at God's Rock?"

Haley said, "He sure did."

"I thought so, but I wasn't in there when he made the announcements." Bonnie turned to Melanie, "Did you enjoy God's Rock?"

Melanie nodded. "But it wasn't what I expected."

Bonnie furrowed her forehead. "What do you mean?"

"Well, the youth pastor was kind of goofy."

The girls tried to stifle their snickering and cast sidelong glances at Bonnie.

Bonnie started to giggle. "He sure is." Her grin widened. "It's one of the many things I love about him."

"Bonnie is Pastor Brett's wife," Cindy explained.

Melanie's face heated. "I'm sorry. I didn't mean . . . "

"I know, don't worry. It's fine." Bonnie giggled again and walked away.

Melanie huffed. "Why didn't you guys warn me?

Haley answered, "How were we supposed to know you were going to say what you did?" She lifted her shoulders. "Besides, Pastor Brett doesn't care. In fact, he probably would consider it a compliment. He loves being crazy."

Ella groaned and clutched her stomach. "I'm starving. I need food!"

Melanie wanted to stay with her friends, but she had to find her mom first. "Sorry, guys I have to leave. My mom said I was supposed to meet her in the fellowship hall."

Ella said, "That's where we're headed."

When they entered the enormous room, Melanie spotted her mom with another woman and waved. She followed the girls as they led the way to the refreshment table. The girls snatched what they wanted from the large assortment of doughnuts, muffins, and danishes. Melanie grabbed a napkin and a brown sugar bear claw.

Rachel joined them.

Haley teased, "It's about time you showed up."

"Hey, I can't help it if our class went longer than yours."

Melanie frowned, puzzled over Rachel's statement.

Rachel explained, "I'm going into the ninth grade. This summer will be my last in God's Rock and my last time going to Junior High camp. Then I'll be off to 4TK, the high school youth group."

Melanie shook her head. "You guys sure have some bizarre names for your youth groups, but they sound kinda cool. What is the high school one called again?"

Rachel raised four fingers. "It's 4TK and it stands for, For the King. It's led by Pastor Cliff."

Melanie continued to question them. “So are all of you going to Junior High camp?” They nodded. “Where is this camp anyway?”

Cindy’s voice was playful. “You’re not going to believe this, but it’s only a couple of miles from your house.”

“Really?” Was this the camp Katie had been wanting her to go to? “What do you do there?”

“Rec,” Ella said, taking another bite out of her blueberry muffin.

“What is rec?”

Ella finished her bite and answered. “Sorry, it’s short for recreation. The leaders split us campers into four teams and we have competitions. It’s wild. We have such a blast.”

“There are other things besides rec.” Rachel counted on her fingers. “There’s archery, canoeing, hiking, and all sorts of games.”

“Sounds like everything you’re describing is recreational activities to me,” Haley razzed. “Anyway, we forgot to tell the mermaid the one thing which will make her want to go more than anything.” She smirked, pausing for dramatic effect. “They have a pool.”

Cindy gushed. “We could all be roommates and Bonnie would be our counselor.” She grabbed Melanie’s arm. “Please say you want to come.”

"Camp does sound like fun, and it would be great to swim every day. But I still don't know." She chewed her lip. "How much is it?"

"Around a few hundred dollars," Rachel said hesitantly.

"Oh! I'll have to ask my parents." Did she really want to go? Definitely. Especially if they had a pool. If her parents had allowed Megan to go to Hawaii, Melanie was sure she could go to camp.

"We'd win the pool competition for sure if we had the mermaid here and JB on our team." Haley bobbed her head and began to strut around like a proud rooster.

The girls cracked up over her antics.

"We should ask Bonnie if they have room or not. Camp does fill up quickly," Rachel said.

"Let me ask my parents first, but I'm sure they'll say yes," said Melanie.

The girls squealed.

Church hadn't been a total waste after all. She'd gotten to know her friends better and had made the decision to go to camp. Things were finally looking up.

8

THE CHOICE

After finishing another slice of pepperoni pizza at the mall, Melanie sipped on a peach-mango smoothie. A large bag at her feet contained her birthday invitations and decorations for her party. They were planning a swim party.

When Mom ate her last bite of pizza, Melanie pulled out the list of all the people she planned to invite. The list included some of her friends from her old school, and her new friends from church and also Vivian and Bonnie. She would have invited her swim team, too, but they had a meet and wouldn't be able to make it. Another name missing was Katie, but she was traveling around the country with her family all summer.

"I wish Katie could come."

"That won't be a problem," Mom said with a mischievous glint in her eyes.

"Why is that?" Melanie's heart gave a hopeful lurch.

"Well, I was going to wait and tell you later but . . . "

"What? Tell me, tell me, tell me!"

"Katie is going to stay with us the weekend of your birthday."

"What? Oh, Mom. Thank you!" Melanie bounded from her chair and practically tackled her mom with a hug. "But I cannot believe Katie kept a secret from me."

"She didn't." Mom chuckled. "She doesn't know yet."

Melanie grinned, "This birthday is going to be even better than I thought it would."

"I'm glad you feel that way, sweetheart. So, other than the party, what do you want your dad and I to get you?"

This was her chance to ask Mom if she could go to camp. "What I really want is kind of expensive."

"At least tell me what it is and allow me to decide if it is too much."

Melanie bit her lip. "I can't believe what I'm going to ask, but I really want to go to the church camp."

"How much is it?"

She gulped. “It’s about a few hundred dollars.”

“Oh,” Mom was quiet. “I’m sorry, sweetheart, but we can’t afford to do both the party and camp. You’ll have to make a choice.”

“But that’s not fair! Megan got to go to Hawaii.”

“We didn’t pay for Megan to go to Hawaii.”

“You didn’t? But you must have given her spending money.”

“Melanie, this isn’t about Megan. It is about how expensive your party will be. We already spent money on the invitations, but we would also need to buy more decorations, food, cake, and other party supplies, plus the added cost of having it at the pool center.”

She really wanted to go to camp, but they had already spent money on her party. “I guess I’ll do the swim party.” Besides, her birthday just wouldn’t be the same if she didn’t have a pool party. There had been enough changes in her life this summer. She didn’t want any more.

Mom reached over and patted her hand. “I’m sorry this is so hard on you. We’ll make sure you can go to camp next year. Now, let’s get going so you can swim while I make the arrangements for your party.”

***

Readjusting her swim cap, Melanie hovered in position over the pool. Diving into a lane, she focused on her strokes and her breathing. She lapped the pool, then shot off toward the other end. Kicking her legs, she coursed through the cool water. When she reached the wall, she pushed off again and continued to make her circuit. After finishing her last lap, Melanie pulled herself out onto the warm cement.

Melanie was winded and she knew if she'd been timed, she would be much slower than usual. It had only been ten days since they moved, and she already felt out of shape. Too bad Dad wasn't here to coach her and cheer her on. It was her last swim of the day, since they were closing off the lap pool for swim team practices. Hopefully next year she would be on one of those teams.

Melanie walked to the lounge chairs, took off her swim cap, removed her ear plugs, and shook out her hair. She wiped herself off with her towel. She sank down and watched as the pool filled with swimmers. There was a group of girls who were about her age. A woman, probably their coach, gathered them together.

After the woman talked with them for a few minutes, the group began to do their warm-ups.

Melanie observed them as they did laps. She judged their technique and tried to determine who was the fastest and which one was best at the breaststroke. She wished she could join them. It would be great to be on a team again.

Melanie turned away. It was only making her upset to watch them. She should focus on her upcoming birthday party. This swim center would be the perfect place. There was the lap pool, an enormous community pool, and a cute baby pool. In the large grassy area, they could set up umbrellas for shade and barbecue hot dogs. It wouldn't be the same as her birthday at home, but it would be close.

Since she couldn't go to camp as her present, she would have to think of something else she wanted for her birthday. She could always use more books, even if her bookcase was a bit overcrowded. Probably clothes, too, since she wouldn't be wearing a uniform to school anymore. It would definitely be a big change, but one she didn't mind.

A whistle blew, drawing her attention back to the swimmers. She really missed her team. Melanie wished she could talk to Katie about everything. Katie would cheer her up. Melanie snickered. Katie would probably even invite her to go to camp.

It was the same camp they had been talking about at church. She had pieced the clues together from the location and the dates. If she'd only said yes, when Katie first asked her. She sighed. It was too late to change her mind. Besides, she really did want to have her pool party. She had already made her decision. It was no use thinking more about it. She would just have to wait until next year. Melanie hoped she wouldn't regret it.

9

FOURTH OF JULY WEEKEND

As Dad drove along the curvy highway, Mom continued enthusiastically, "Shannon and I went to high school together. Of course, she wasn't Shannon Barrett back then." Mom turned. "And Mel, Shannon has a son about your age. He swims, too."

From the backseat, Melanie replied, "Let me guess. His name is JB." She rolled her eyes. "Yeah, Cindy and the other girls told me about him, too." Who cared about some boy when she could swim? Unless . . . the face of the cute boy from youth group popped into her head. It would be so cool if he was there today. Melanie smiled to herself.

At church last Sunday, Shannon had invited their family for a Fourth of July barbecue. Melanie hadn't been thrilled about it, until she found out the Barretts had a pool. She could swim all day if she wanted. Plus, Mom had said her friends might be there. And it was even better to have Dad home, too.

From the front of the property, the house seemed small, hidden behind overgrown trees and shrubbery. On the front porch, they could see into the house through the screen. Dad rang the doorbell, and someone called out, "Come in."

They strolled in.

The lady, who Mom had been talking to in the fellowship hall last Sunday, greeted them. Shannon was only a couple inches taller than Melanie, with kind blue eyes and short, tawny hair. Mom made the introductions and Shannon led them to the back deck.

The deck was packed with people and had two tables loaded with food. Three barbecues filled the air with the aroma of grilled meats and smoke. Melanie viewed the yard from the railing. It looked like a park rather than someone's backyard, with its large expanse of grass. There were groups playing volleyball, frisbee, and horseshoes. And the pool was enormous, plenty of room for practicing laps. But not today, since it was so crowded. Too bad. But before she could be disappointed, she spotted her friends lounging at the edge of the pool.

Melanie grabbed a quick bite. She was here to swim, not to eat. Hoisting her bag of clothes on her shoulder, she made her way back into the house and down the hallway. She couldn't remember which door Shannon had said the bathroom would be.

Oops, wrong door.

She stopped in her tracks because the room she had almost entered was definitely a boy's room with its blue paint and the walls plastered with posters of athletes. Trophies, mostly for swimming, and ribbons overcrowded the shelves of the bookcase. Mom and her friends weren't kidding when they said JB was a swimmer.

She heard a noise and turned. Melanie's heart quickened and her eyes widened. It was the cute boy.

"Hi," they both said at the same time, and then laughed awkwardly.

He broke the silence. "Didn't I see you last week at God's Rock?"

"Yeah," Melanie said shyly.

"Um, I'm glad you came. I was hoping to meet you," he stammered.

"You were?"

The cute boy rushed on. “You’re Melanie, right?”

She nodded. “So you must be . . . ?”

His face reddened. “Oh, sorry. I’m JB.”

“Oh, so this is your room. I didn’t mean to . . . I was just, um . . . ” How was she supposed to tell him she was looking for the bathroom?

“The bathroom is the next door. Don’t worry, lots of people get confused. I’m mean, uh, I’m just assuming.”

“Yeah, thanks.”

“Cindy said you’re a great swimmer.”

“I am pretty good.” She grinned. “But I don’t think I have as many trophies as you.” She shrugged. “But it really doesn’t matter to me. I just love being in the water.”

“Me, too.”

Shannon’s voice yelled from the other room. “JB, I need those towels.”

He smiled, “I better not keep my mom waiting much longer. Well, I guess I’ll see you in the pool.” He went to the end of the hall to the closet.

Melanie found the bathroom and changed. She headed to the pool to join her friends. Leaning back on her palms in her blue one-piece bathing suit, she soaked in the warm sun as she listened to her friends chatting away.

"Hey, girl." A boy with dark hair stood in the pool close to them. It took Melanie a few moments to realize the boy was talking to her. "I hear you're a pretty good swimmer. Want to race?" he challenged.

Melanie rolled her eyes. "Not with you."

He clutched his chest. "Oh, I'm so hurt. What are you, chicken or something?"

JB stood next to him. "Leave her alone, Adam."

"But you said she was good."

"Yeah, but she doesn't need to prove it," he answered.

Cindy interjected. "Adam, it is pretty brave of you to challenge Melanie, since I am sure she would beat you."

Adam glared at her and then swam away. JB smiled at Melanie, then joined Adam.

Haley said, "So, mermaid, aren't you going to get in the water?"

"I'd like to, but there isn't much room to do any real swimming."

"But we need you to practice so our team at camp will win the swim competition." Haley grinned.

Melanie bit her lip and frowned.

Cindy understood instantly. "Oh no," she groaned. "You aren't going to camp, are you?"

Melanie shook her head.

The other girls added their displeasure.

Bonnie came over and scooted herself next to Melanie.

The girls fell silent.

"Was I interrupting something?" Bonnie asked.

"No," Cindy blurted. "We were talking about camp. And we just found out Melanie can't go."

Melanie wanted to give them some sort of explanation. "I already talked to my mom. I had to choose between camp or having a birthday party. I can do both next year. Oh." She slapped her forehead. "I just remembered I forgot to bring my birthday invitations."

Bonnie offered, "You know, I could talk to your parents about camp. We have a fundraiser coming up which could cover some of the cost."

Melanie remembered how upset her dad had been when Megan had suggested they borrow money from their grandparents. He was adamant about providing for the family himself. He probably wouldn't want her to participate in a fundraiser. "No, thank you. I'll just go next year."

A wave of water washed over the girls and they squealed. All of them were soaked. Pastor Brett's head emerged from the pool, where the splash had come from.

Bonnie yelled, "Brett, I'm going to get you for that."

She dove into the pool. Melanie laughed, then followed her.

***

It was Sunday morning and Mom had made them waffles for breakfast. Their weekend had been filled with family fun. First, the barbecue on Friday. Then Saturday they had spent all day together: shopping, swimming, and seeing a movie. They were missing church and normally Melanie wouldn't mind, but she had hoped to pass out her birthday invitations. Now she would have to go to God's Rock on Wednesday night to do it.

As Mom cleared away the dishes, Dad reached for his briefcase. Melanie groaned. If Dad was going to work, she would have gone to church with Vivian.

Dad cleared his throat. "We've been so busy this weekend, I almost forgot to share my news. I've started looking for apartments for us." He pulled brochures out of his briefcase. "Every one of them has a pool, Mel. I wanted to make sure our mermaid has one to practice in."

Melanie bit her lip as she scanned the colorful pamphlets. Were they really moving back? She was getting what she wanted, but now she would miss her new friends: Cindy's constant chatter, Haley's merciless teasing, Ella's insatiable hunger, and Rachel's quiet smiles.

"Daddy, I'm so glad we'll be together again. I miss you so much. But do we have to move back? I know it's only been a couple of weeks, but I really like living here."

"I thought you would be excited to move back, especially when you found out about the pool." He turned to Mom. "What do you think, Gretchen?"

"Jack, you already know how I feel. I wanted to give living up here a chance." She tilted her head and pressed her lips together.

He exhaled a deep breath. "I know you did, but I don't see how we can do it. I know we thought I might be able to do some contract work here, but there's no room in this cabin for an office. And I want to be with my girls." He reached out and grabbed their hands. "I can't give up this job. It's what we've needed so I can really provide for our family again."

Melanie squeezed his hand. She didn't know what they would do. No matter what they chose, she'd be losing something.

10

DISAPPOINTMENTS

At God's Rock all Melanie wanted to do was be with her friends and pass out her birthday invitations. She made her way to the couch, where they had sat last time, but none of her friends were there. Cindy and Ella would probably be late, but where were Haley and Rachel? She sat down alone and bit her lip.

She didn't have long to wait for youth group to begin. In what must be his usual manner, Pastor Brett bounded on stage. He grinned broadly. "I'm happy to announce with our fundraiser on Saturday, we were able to raise about seven thousand dollars for camp costs." Applause and some whoops came from the kids around her. Pastor Brett continued, "Camp is only a few weeks away, so make sure you get your medical permission slips to me or Bonnie. And, for those of you who are planning on signing up for paintball or zip-lining . . . "

Melanie stopped listening. She wished she didn't have to hear about it. Why did it bother her so much? That was a dumb question. She knew why. It was because she really wanted to go. But it was too late. She had already chosen her birthday party. Across the room she noticed JB. Was he going to camp? Probably.

"We're going to do something a little different tonight." Melanie raised her head as Pastor Brett spoke. "We're going to have a game, so let's head over to the gym."

There were mixed reactions as Melanie followed everyone else and was the last one out of the youth room. When she exited, Cindy grabbed her arm. "Finally."

"What do you mean, finally? I've been waiting for you," Melanie accused her with a smile.

"Oh, well our family is usually late. It's a family trait except for my brother, Trevor. Since we're friends, you're going to have to get used to it," Cindy teased.

"I brought my birthday invitations. Where is everybody?"

Cindy shrugged. "I don't know, but where's mine?"

"It's in my pocket. I'll give it to you after."

"I can't wait." She squeezed Melanie's arm.

After a tiring but fun game, they headed over to the side of the gym to pick up Melanie's sweatshirt and get out the invitations. When Melanie pulled them out, someone bumped into her and she collided roughly with Cindy, dropping the invitations on the floor. It was Adam, the boy who had challenged her to a swim contest at the barbecue.

"Excuse you." He sneered and looked at the floor. "Now, what do we have here?" He purposely ground his foot into the envelopes. All her pristine white envelopes were crushed and marked with Adam's shoe prints. Then he picked up one and started opening it.

Cindy snatched it out of his hands. "I'll take that. It doesn't have your name on it."

Melanie's eyes welled up with tears.

Cindy exclaimed, "Adam, you're such a . . . "

"Such a what?" He glared.

"Never mind."

He strutted away, smirking.

Cindy balled up her fists. "If he wasn't a friend of JB's, I'd let him have it." She said, through clenched teeth. "He makes me so mad!" She knelt to retrieve the damaged birthday invitations.

Melanie couldn't hold back the tears. They slipped down her cheeks. She bit her lip and fled. She kept her head down so no one would see she was crying, especially Adam. In the hallway, she glanced up and caught sight of JB coming toward her. His eyes widened. Melanie looked away and walked as quickly as she could to the restroom.

She slammed through the entrance and went straight into a stall. She blew her nose, but it was useless to wipe away her tears since she couldn't stop crying. The squeak of the door and hushed voices warned Melanie she was no longer alone.

Bonnie's concerned voice asked, "Melanie, are you okay?"

Melanie sniffed and heard Cindy explain to Bonnie what had happened. When she had finished, Melanie came out.

"I'm so sorry, Melanie." Bonnie patted her arm and rolled her eyes. "Boys," she huffed.

Melanie couldn't help herself and burst out laughing. So did Bonnie and Cindy.

Bonnie smiled. "Now, that's better."

"It's just . . . I was hoping to pass out my invitations tonight. But Adam ruined them, now I'll have to start over." She bit her lip.

Bonnie volunteered. "I'm crafty. I can make new envelopes for you, and if you'd like I can mail them out, too."

"Really?"

"Of course, really. It would be my pleasure. I just need a list."

Cindy grinned. "I'm RSVPing right now. I'm definitely going to your party."

Melanie spoke hesitantly. "Bonnie, I was going to invite you, too, but I wasn't sure you'd want to come to a kid's party."

"We would love to come. I'll just have to check our calendar."

"Who's we?"

"Pastor Brett and me. Is that okay?"

"Ah, well, it's kind of a girls-only swim party. The only guy who will be there is my dad."

"If that is the case, maybe I won't tell him." She winked.

Melanie interrupted. "No, he can come. It's no big deal. Just as long as he doesn't do cannonballs in the pool."

Bonnie chuckled. "I can't make any promises."

They laughed.

"Do you mind if I pray with you?" Bonnie asked.

Melanie shrugged. Cindy smiled and put her arm across Melanie's shoulder and bowed her head.

"God, Melanie's having a rough time. You know all about it and what she is struggling with. Help her adjust to the changes in her life. Help her not be disappointed when things don't go as she expected them to. Give her peace. Show her how much You love and care about her, even in the little things in life. In Jesus' name, amen."

Cindy squeezed her shoulder. Melanie felt better, but she wished JB hadn't seen her crying.

"I'll be praying for you, Melanie." Bonnie held up the invitations. "And I'll get to working on these right away. They'll be in the mail tomorrow."

"Thank you." Melanie didn't know if the prayer would work, but it was nice knowing people cared about her. Things seemed to be looking better already.

11

A CHANGE OF HEART

Even though Melanie had felt better after attending God's Rock on Wednesday, she didn't know if she could face church anytime soon. Guilt nagged at her, since Bonnie had been so nice and had taken care of her birthday invitations. But the incident with Adam kept replaying in her mind, and she couldn't stop wondering what JB thought when he'd seen her crying. And she'd have to hear about camp again. Her decision was made. She wouldn't be going with Mom this morning.

When Mom came out of her room, Melanie lifted her chin and stated, "I'm not going to church."

"Are you feeling okay?"

"I'm fine," she answered tersely. Her tone wasn't what she intended, but she continued anyway. "I just don't want to go, and I'm almost thirteen, which makes me old enough to stay home by myself."

Mom tilted her head and raised her eyebrows. "I know things haven't been easy, but I don't appreciate you speaking to me in that way. You don't have to go, but we'll talk about this when I get home."

Melanie nodded and bit her lip, trying to keep her tears from spilling.

Mom checked her watch. "I'd better hurry or I'll be late."

Just as Mom closed the door, Melanie ran into her room, threw herself across her bed, and cried. Her frustrations and pain poured out. Why had she taken this out on Mom? Mom had no idea what had happened at God's Rock. It wasn't her fault. Melanie was so confused.

After Melanie's tears stopped, Bonnie's prayer about how God loved and cared for her came to mind. But how could He love her especially with the way she'd been acting? Bonnie had also said something about God giving her peace. That's what she really needed. How could she get that peace? What would Katie tell her?

She knew exactly what Katie would say. She would tell her to pray. It was worth a shot.

"Okay, God, here goes." She took a deep breath. "Please show me that You love and care for me. Give me peace. Amen."

Her prayer sounded more like she was making demands on God. She shook her head. Couldn't she do anything right? Calmness came over her, comforting her aching heart. She sighed and fell asleep.

***

In the afternoon, Mom walked through the doorway, carrying their lunch. She dropped it on the counter.

Melanie hugged her. "I'm so sorry, Mom."

Mom squeezed her back. "I know, Sweetheart. Why don't we talk about it while we eat? I got your favorite, a hot ham and cheese sandwich."

Melanie unwrapped the sub and licked off some of the melted Swiss cheese from her finger. She looked up. Mom's eyes were red and puffy. "Mom, have you been crying? Did something happen at church?"

"Yes, but it was the good kind of crying. You know, when you're happy. I'm fine. But what I really want to know is what happened this morning?"

Melanie flopped down into a chair at the dining room table. She didn't really want to talk about it, but she did owe Mom an explanation. Between bites of her sandwich, Melanie told her about the incident with Adam at God's Rock.

When she finished, Mom asked, "Why didn't you tell me?"

"I guess because I was embarrassed. I'm still embarrassed. I did feel better about it after Bonnie and Cindy prayed with me." She paused. "But I don't think it was just about Adam." Melanie bit her lip. "It's hard to go to church because everyone is talking about going to camp."

"And you're disappointed you can't go."

She nodded. Mom started to console her, but Melanie interrupted. "It's all right. I feel better now. Something happened after you left." Melanie was hesitant. What would Mom think about her praying? She decided to jump right in. "I asked God to show me He loved and cared for me and to give me peace. And I think He did. At least, the peace part. I felt better after praying." Melanie shrugged. "And then I fell asleep."

Mom reached over and squeezed Melanie's hand. Tears rolled down her cheeks. "I experienced something similar at church this morning. I asked Jesus to forgive my sins and become Lord of my life. Now I have peace and a new relationship with God."

"Oh." What did she mean? Was it the answer to finding the peace she'd been asking for? But if it was, why would Mom be crying? This whole God thing was strange. "Why are you crying then?"

"Because I am so happy, and I feel . . . oh, I don't know how to describe it. I feel complete, as if a hole in my heart has been filled."

Melanie tentatively smiled. "That's great." Even to her own ears, she didn't sound very convincing.

Mom squeezed her hand again, and then let go. She wiped her eyes and switched the subject. "All of your friends practically tackled me at church wanting to know where you were, and RSVPing for your party."

Melanie's eyes bulged. "Who? Who can come?"

"All of them."

"Woo hoo!" Melanie hollered. "Are you sure?"

Mom nodded. "Yes, I even wrote down their names." She pulled the list from her purse and read the names aloud. "That Haley girl is quite the character. She kept asking about you. 'Where's our mermaid?' and 'When can we see our mermaid?'" Mom smiled. "It was very sweet. You've made some really special friends."

Melanie nodded.

"Bonnie was concerned about you, too. She was hoping to see you today. She told me she and Brett are coming to the party." Mom frowned. "If I had known she had fixed the invitations and mailed them for us, I would have thanked her. No more keeping secrets like that again, young lady."

"I won't. So, when are we getting the decorations and the goodies for the gift bags?"

"Sometime this week. I was planning on getting a few other things as well. Which reminds me, I had an idea. Would you like to help me make an office upstairs for Dad?"

"In the loft?"

"In a way, but I was actually thinking about the storage closet. It's large and has shelves, a light, and a door. The boxes need to be cleaned out, sorted through, and organized. It's a big job."

"Would that mean Dad could work up here and live with us?"

"I don't know, but it's what I'm hoping."

"Then I'm in."

12

ACCIDENT

In Vivian's aviary, Melanie tried a birdcall by sucking her lips together. It sounded more like a high-pitched kiss, but Paco loved it and chirped back to her. She called to him and he immediately flew down, landing on her outstretched hand. Paco scrambled up across Melanie's shoulder and hid underneath her hair. His feathers tickled the back of her neck. She giggled.

"I've been thinking about asking my parents for my own bird for my birthday. But I'm not sure, since I don't know if I could find one, I like as much as Paco. Plus, I did some research online and grey-cheeked parakeets are expensive. They're relatively rare."

"Yes, I got Paco from a friend who really couldn't give him the attention he needed. He's been happy here, but he is even more so when you're around.

Melanie continued excitedly. "It said they are very affectionate birds, but I already knew that. I learned, too, they're good mimics and some can even talk."

"My Sheba knows a few words. But she only talks when she feels like it, usually when she is in a good mood."

When Sheba heard her name, she squawked, "Sheba's a pretty bird."

Both Melanie and Vivian laughed.

Melanie pursed her lips together. "I was wondering, would you mind if I taught Paco some tricks?"

"Of course, you may."

"Cool. I really would love it if I could teach him to talk. But there are a couple of other things I'd like him to learn, too."

"We should go to the pet store and get him some treats to reward him," Vivian suggested.

"Yes, that's a great idea. It reminds me though, Mom wanted me to ask if you'd like to go out to lunch with us today. We'll be stopping by the mall, too. We need to buy more stuff for my party and some office supplies as a surprise for my dad."

"Sure. Sounds like fun. What's the surprise for your dad?"

"It's my mom's idea. We've been cleaning out the storage closet to make an office for him. We're almost finished."

"I'm sure he will appreciate all your hard work. When does your mom want to leave?"

"Anytime you're ready."

"We can go after you're done playing with Paco."

Melanie could spend all day with Paco if Vivian let her. But she could hardly wait to get the stuff for her party. She pointed to a branch and commanded the parakeet, "Paco, perch." Paco flew off to the tree.

Once Vivian got her purse, they walked over to Melanie's house. It was a perfect summer day. A warm breeze carried the scent of redwood trees. She could hear the trickling creek and the birds trilling. She missed Paco already. On the back porch, Melanie opened the screen door and stepped into the hallway.

"Mom, Vivian said yes." She called out.

Her eyes adjusted to the light inside and she saw Mom unconscious and lying awkwardly at the bottom of the stairs.

"Mom!" Melanie rushed over to her and knelt down. She then noticed Mom's ankle twisted oddly.

Vivian came beside her. "Gretchen, are you okay?"

Mom didn't respond.

Everything began to slow down. Melanie's pulse roared in her ears. What were they going to do? Would her mom wake up? God, please don't let her die. Her vision blurred from her tears.

"Melanie!"

"What?" Melanie shook her head.

"Listen carefully," Vivian instructed. "I know you're upset, but you need to be strong. Your mother needs our help. Take a deep breath, dry your eyes, and do as I say. Can you do that?"

Melanie nodded through her tears.

"Good. Now call 9-1-1, and then bring the phone to me. You can do this Melanie." Vivian patted her.

Melanie cautiously climbed over Mom and went for the phone. God, please help my mom. Melanie's hands shook as she dialed the number.

"9-1-1, what is your emergency?"

"Um," Melanie's voice quivered, "my mom's hurt. She fell down the stairs. We just found her." She walked toward Vivian. Her legs felt like logs.

"Is your mom awake?" The operator spoke patiently.

"No, but Vivian will know more. I'm giving the phone to her."

Vivian cradled the receiver as she spoke to the operator. After a couple of minutes, she placed the phone down and turned to Melanie. "We'll try to keep your mom comfortable. The ambulance is on its way."

Vivian kept Melanie busy gathering what they needed for the trip to the hospital. Mom still hadn't woken up. Hopefully help would be here soon. She heard sirens in the distance.

13

HOSPITAL

Melanie paced back and forth along the beige tile floor in the hospital waiting room. Her knees wobbled and finally she dropped down into a chair. "I can't stand this anymore. I wish they would let me see her." She wrung her hands. They had been told Mom had a concussion and a possible broken ankle, but they would have to wait for Dad to find out more.

"Be patient, Melanie. Your dad will be here soon." Vivian patted her hand.

Melanie could feel the fear and frustration building up inside her. She bit her lip.

Vivian put her arm around her and squeezed her shoulder. "It's going to be all right."

Melanie heard the sliding door of the entrance. She looked up, hoping it was Dad. It wasn't him. It was Bonnie.

Bonnie hurried over to them. "How are you doing, Melanie?"

Melanie's mouth trembled. "What are you doing here?"

"Vivian called, and I thought you might need me." Bonnie directed the remainder of her reply to Vivian. "I called Shannon and she is setting up the dinners, but we'll need to talk to Jack or Gretchen to see when they want them to start, and, of course, I started the prayer chain."

"What are you talking about?" Melanie asked.

Bonnie squeezed her hand. "Our church wants to help. We're arranging meals for your family. So your mom can rest when she gets home."

Melanie gave a tentative smile. "Oh, thank you. What's the chain thing you were talking about?"

"It's called a prayer chain," Bonnie explained. "It's like when you play telephone, but we use it with prayer. I call the first person on the prayer chain and tell them the prayer request. They pray, and then call the next person. By the time it's done, most of the church will be praying for your mom and your family."

It was nice to know so many people cared about her and her family. This was a new experience. Usually her family was on its own, keeping things together without any outside help. She always knew she could count on Katie, but her parents only had each other. Now, they had Vivian, Bonnie, Shannon, and the people at church.

A sense of relief washed over her. They didn't have to do this alone.

Bonnie pulled out some playing cards from her purse. "Want to play a game?"

Melanie nodded. Anything to distract her from the waiting.

***

"Hi, mermaid."

Melanie looked up, threw down her cards, jumped up, and hugged her dad.

He put his arms around her and kissed the top of her head. "It's going to be okay," he said soothingly. He turned to Vivian. "How is Gretchen doing?"

"Nothing has changed since I updated you last," Vivian answered.

"I think I'd like to go and see her now." He released Melanie. "I'll be back in a bit."

He and Vivian went to the nurse's station. A little while later, he was back. Melanie was waiting for him this time.

His face was expressionless as he walked over to them. "She's awake, but groggy. They're going to take her over for X-rays to see if her ankle is broken. From what the doctor thinks, it probably is. Mel, Mom told me to tell you she loves you and she is proud of you. She doesn't want you to worry about her."

Dad extended his hand to Bonnie. "I don't think we've been introduced, even though I saw you with Melanie at the barbecue. I'm Jack."

"I'm Bonnie." She smiled, returning his hand shake.

Melanie added. "She's my Sunday school teacher."

He nodded. "Thank you for being here for my daughter."

"You're welcome."

Dad turned to Vivian. "Thank you so much Vivian for all you did. I hope it isn't too much to ask, but could Melanie spend the night with you? I'm going to be spending the night here with Gretchen."

"Of course, it's no trouble."

Melanie argued, "But I want to stay with you. Can't I see Mom?"

"Melanie it would be best if you went with Vivian. The doctor assured me we'll most likely be taking your mother home tomorrow. You can see her then."

Melanie bit her lip. She wanted to scream. Why couldn't she visit Mom? Why didn't she have any say in what was happening anymore? It just wasn't fair.

***

On the drive home, Vivian asked, "Do you want to stop and get something to eat?"

"No."

"Okay, well how about when we get home? We'll make spaghetti for dinner. How does that sound?"

Melanie shrugged. "I'm not really hungry." She didn't want to go to Vivian's house. What she wanted was to be with Mom and Dad.

Vivian was quiet for a few moments and then spoke. "I know today was really hard for you, but you were very brave and a great help to your mom and to me. If you want to talk about it, I'm here for you."

Melanie swallowed hard. "I do want to talk about it. Mostly, I don't understand how Mom got hurt."

"She fell down the stairs. Accidents happen."

"No, I didn't mean that. I meant . . . well, she became a Christian on Sunday and now this? Isn't God supposed to protect her, or something? Why did

He let this happen to her? I even prayed God would show me He loves and cares for me, but then Mom gets hurt. I just don't get it."

Vivian tilted her head. "That is a difficult and complicated question." She was silent for a few moments. "God does protect us, Melanie, but that doesn't mean nothing bad will ever happen to us."

"What about the verse they talked about in God's Rock? The one about God working the good out for people?"

"You mean Romans 8:28? 'And we know that God causes all things to work together for good to those who love God, to those who are called according to His purpose.'"

"Yeah, that's the one."

"That's not exactly what it means. It's a promise when we love and follow God, that no matter what happens to us, good or bad, God will bring good from it. I've seen it in my own life."

Melanie crossed her arms. "Well, what about my mom? What is good about that?" Her voice trembled.

"We don't know the answer right now, and we may not see the good yet. But I know we will." She paused. "Melanie, I'm going to challenge you. I want you to figure out what good comes out of this."

"But how will the promise work for me if I don't believe?"

"Your mom and I do. Also, I believe God will want to show you the good He can do in your life, too."

Melanie gave a half shrug. "I guess."

If God could make something good come out of this mess, then she was all for it. *Okay, God, let's see what You can do.*

14

HARD CHOICES

As soon as Mom arrived home, there was a steady stream of visitors. Shannon had arranged meals to be delivered every day by different members of the church. The first meal had been provided by the head pastor and his wife. They would have plenty of food for weeks.

The guests were thoughtful, but it was tiring Mom out. Mom really needed sleep to heal from her concussion and broken ankle. Dad and Melanie tried to keep the house as quiet as possible and they did their best to make Mom comfortable.

Melanie hated to watch her mom in pain. Melanie knew what she should do, but she continued to wrestle with the idea. She didn't want to cancel her party, but she had to. There was no way Mom could finish planning her party and Melanie couldn't do it herself. There was no other choice.

"Dad, I need to talk to you and Mom. It's important."

"Sure, Mel."

Melanie entered her parent's room followed by her dad. She lowered herself onto the bed beside Mom. Dread pooled in her stomach. This was going to be harder than she thought. She took a deep breath and plowed in. "I've made a decision. I'm going to cancel my party."

"What? No." They both said.

Melanie reached for Mom's hand. "Mom, you really scared me. You're more important to me than a party. It's just too much right now. I've already made up my mind. But there's one thing I'm not sure I can do." She paused. "Can someone else call my friends and cancel?" Melanie bit her lip to keep from crying.

Mom squeezed her hand. "I'll call your school friends, and I'll find someone to help me get in touch with your new church friends."

"Thanks, Mom. I was also wondering would you mind if Katie still came up. Would that be too much for you, Mom?" She hastily added, "I'll even clean my room."

Mom gave a soft chuckle. "Then how can I refuse? Yes, Katie can stay with us."

Even though it twisted her heart, Melanie continued. "I was also thinking I should take a break from swimming. It's too much trouble to find someone to take me to the pool."

Mom's voice had a slight tremor in it. "Melanie, are you sure? You seem to be giving up so much."

"I might start swimming again someday, but right now is not the time for it."

Tears ran down Mom's face. "My baby is growing up. Being so responsible." She wiped her eyes.

Dad scowled. "I don't like this. If we had our own place, I would move both of you down with me today. But maybe we could find a hotel with a pool until we find an apartment. That way, our mermaid can keep swimming and I'll have my girls with me, except for Megan."

Mom shook her head. "I want to stay, Jack. Here, not in a cramped hotel room."

"Who's going to take care of you?" Dad argued.

"I will." Melanie piped in.

Mom smiled at her. "Yes, Melanie will take care of me. Vivian is next door if we need her. We have plenty of food and we've had multiple volunteers from the church who are willing to take me to any doctor appointments I might have."

He frowned. "I wish I could quit, but we need the money even more with the hospital bills."

"Jack, why not look for another job while you're here? I've been worried about you. You've been working so hard—too hard in fact. We really miss you, and I want a job for you that you enjoy and isn't so stressful. One that gives us time together."

Dad came over and hugged them both. "I'll try. I think I would enjoy living here. It's so . . . so peaceful. And, Gretchen, these new friends you've made, these church people are different from what I expected. They care about us and are so supportive, helping us in our time of need."

Mom nodded.

"And Gretchen, I've noticed a change in you. You seem, well, happy and content. I don't know if it's this place or you going to church."

A light came into her eyes. "I believe it is the new relationship I have with Jesus and what I've been learning about God."

Dad looked puzzled, then shrugged. "Well, now that you believe in praying, maybe you should ask the big guy upstairs if He can find me a new job."

"I already have been." She reached for his hand. "And Jack, we'll support you no matter what. If you don't get a new job, then we'll move back at the end of the summer."

He nodded. "I'm sorry I haven't been here for you girls like I should. But I promise I'll be coming home every weekend, which includes taking you swimming, Mel." He patted Melanie's hand. "Don't worry, sweetheart, we'll think of something to make your birthday special. It's only once in a lifetime you turn thirteen." Dad grimaced, "I can't believe I'll have two teenage daughters."

Melanie grinned. "I'll never be too old for you to be my daddy."

"So, Mermaid, want to help me finish up the office?"

"How did you find out? It was supposed to be our surprise for you." Melanie pursed her lips.

"Your mom definitely made it a surprise, but not one I want repeated." Dad chuckled and he and Melanie headed upstairs.

A few minutes later, Mom called to her. Melanie went back to her parent's room. "What's up, Mom?"

"It's all set. Vivian will take care of getting ahold of all the girls. She just needs a list. She also mentioned she would like to do a family birthday dinner for you at her house. How does that sound?"

Melanie grinned. "Great." And she meant it.

"And some chocolate cupcakes, too."

"Even better." Maybe things would improve around here. She could only hope.

15

UNEXPECTED VISITORS

In the afternoon, there was loud thumping on the screen door. Melanie put down her book and answered it. Shannon stood on their front step carrying a casserole dish in her oven-mitten covered hands.

Shannon held up the dish. "We're the dinner crew tonight." Behind her, JB lifted grocery bags out of their van.

Melanie stepped aside and held the screen door open. She gulped and tried to act normal. The last time she'd seen JB, she'd been crying. Why couldn't she just disappear?

JB smiled at her as he walked through the door. Melanie bit her lip.

Shannon called from the kitchen. "JB, could you please bring in the cooler and don't forget those bags in the back. Melanie, he's going to need some help."

For JB and Melanie, there were multiple trips to the van. They carried in load after load. The pile grew larger and larger until the kitchen counter was completely covered. It looked as though Shannon had been on a shopping spree.

Mom asked from her spot on the couch, "Is there anything I can do?"

Shannon ordered, "Gretchen, you just stay where you are. I have everything taken care of." She sorted through the contents. "Melanie honey, I'd appreciate if you'd help with putting away the groceries."

Mom tried to position herself so she could watch what they were doing. "Shannon, you've spent way too much."

"I only bought a few grocery items. The rest are things for you to borrow, since I knew you would be cooped up for a while. I have books, movies, puzzles, and craft books with supplies. Plenty of activities you can do without getting up." Shannon turned toward Melanie. "I brought some books for you, too, Melanie. That is, if you like to read. It's some of the books I read as a young girl and some of my daughter's books, as well. You might even like the ones I brought for your mom, too."

"I love to read. Thank you. And it will be fun working on some craft projects with Mom."

After they had the kitchen organized, Shannon instructed Melanie on how to heat up the enchiladas that she had prepared for their dinner. Melanie's mouth watered. Shannon had thought of everything: shredded cheese, sour cream, and olives for the toppings. For the side dishes, they would have refried beans and Spanish ricc.

Shannon said to Mom, "I hope you don't mind if we stay for a visit, too, Gretchen. I'm on my way to take JB to swim practice, but we don't have to leave for a while."

Mom beamed. "That would be lovely. Melanie, why don't you go outside and show JB the creek?"

Melanie turned to JB, who was standing by the dining room table with his hands in his pockets. "Want to see it?"

"Sure." JB followed her down the hallway.

Melanie cringed. To get to the back door, they would need to pass her room. She'd forgotten how messy it was. Melanie raced ahead of him, but when she got to her door to close it, her clothes were in the way. Before she could kick them aside, he had caught up to her.

He stopped and glanced in.

Melanie blushed. "I wasn't expecting company. At least, no one who would see my room anyway."

He shrugged. "My room isn't always clean. But I disagree with you."

Melanie raised her eyebrows. "What? My room isn't messy?"

JB laughed. "No, your room is . . . anything I say . . . um, never mind." He pursed his lips. "Actually, I was talking about your trophies. You have more than me."

"Yeah, right." Melanie huffed. "I don't have nearly as many as you do." She shook her head.

They walked out the back door and down to the creek. In the sunlight, she noticed the freckles which sprinkled his nose and cheeks. JB had really long eyelashes and his eyebrows were so light she could barely see them. Melanie's forehead crinkled. She hadn't noticed it before, but he was wearing a ring on the fourth finger of his left hand. That was strange, since he definitely wasn't married. What was that about?

He jumped down to the edge of the water, surveying the creek.

Melanie asked, "What are you looking for? I don't usually see very many fish."

"Water bugs."

"Oh, you mean water skitters?"

"I've never heard that name for them before."

"That's what my mom calls them."

"You're lucky. Having a creek in your backyard is so cool."

"Yeah." She gave a half shrug. "But I'd rather have a pool like you. We had a pool at our old house, so I swam every day."

"No wonder you're such a great swimmer." He lifted his head and smiled.

"My mom was taking me swimming at the pool in town, but she can't now."

"You can swim all you want at camp."

"I'm not going. I had to choose between a birthday party or camp. Now I can't have either."

"That's rough." He stuck his hands in his pockets.

Melanie frowned and was quiet.

"I didn't mean to make you upset," JB apologized. "Are you mad at me?"

"No, it's just . . . " Melanie bit her lip. She would not let him see her cry again.

He spoke hesitantly. “I think what you did was very brave.”

Melanie gulped. “What?” She didn’t trust herself to say more.

“When your mom got hurt, it must’ve been scary seeing her at the bottom of the stairs. To help like you did, that takes courage.”

“I was just so glad Vivian was there. She was the one who told me what to do.”

“I’m sure you helped more than you realize. Pastor Brett prayed for your mom at God’s Rock and in Sunday school. Actually, a lot of people at church have been praying for your mom.” He cleared his throat. “Including me.”

She smiled. “Thanks, that was really nice of you. Well, it’s nice of everyone.” Her hands began to sweat. Melanie changed the subject. “So, you have a sister. Any brothers?”

“Nope, just two sisters.”

“Older or younger?”

“One of each.”

“I have an older sister, Megan. We’re nothing alike. She’s a cheerleader and looks exactly like my mom. She’s so popular and pretty but really bossy.”

JB looked down. “You’re probably more alike than you think.” He blushed.

What did he mean by that?

16

BIRTHDAY SURPRISE

Melanie paced the living room. With every circuit she peered out the window watching for Dad and Katie to arrive. She knew traffic would be horrible for them on a Friday night. She exhaled. Cleaning her room hadn't taken that long and her bag was packed, since Katie and she were going to spend the night at Vivian's. Melanie had hoped she could play with Paco, but Mom had refused. It was her birthday, but it hadn't been much fun so far.

A car door slammed, and Melanie raced to the front door. Katie bounded in and both girls squealed and threw their arms around each other.

"Happy Birthday, Mel!" Katie grinned, taking in the surroundings. "I can't believe I'm here."

Dad interrupted, "Where's my birthday girl?"

"Right here." Melanie hugged him as he kissed the top of her head.

"I can't believe my baby girl is a teenager." His arms tightened around her, then he released her. "Now, let's not keep Vivian waiting."

Katie's smile broadened. "I can't wait." She clapped her hands.

Going out the back door, the girls each carried their own overnight bag, pillow, and sleeping bag. After Dad got Mom down from the porch and into her wheelchair, he pushed her up the path. Melanie led the way.

When she reached Vivian's back door, Melanie hesitated. She had never been downstairs at Vivian's house. "Are you sure we're supposed to come in this way?"

Mom insisted. "Vivian said she would leave it unlocked for us and to come right in."

It was difficult for Melanie to turn the knob, since her arms were full. She slowly opened the door and stepped through. "Hello?" The house was dark.

Suddenly, the lights turned on. "Surprise!"

Her friends from church leapt out from behind the furniture. Cindy, Haley, Rachel, Ella, Bonnie, and Vivian all grinned at her.

Melanie dropped her things in shock. Her heart pounded. After catching her breath, she was able to speak. "Wow, I can't believe it."

Mom smiled. "Blame Vivian. She planned it all."

"Bonnie helped, too," Vivian added.

Katie wiped her forehead with the back of her hand. "Phew, I'm so glad that's over. It's been so hard keeping a secret from you, even if it was only for a few minutes."

Two voices yelled, "Katie." Haley and Ella ran over and hugged Katie.

Melanie asked, "How do you know each other?"

"From camp," they said in unison and laughed.

Melanie bit her lip. Oh, how she wished she could go to camp, too. But she refused to be upset about it. This was her surprise party, and she wasn't going to allow anything to spoil it. In the corner, there was a pile of sleeping bags, pillows, and overnight bags. "Yay, a slumber party!"

The downstairs family room and kitchenette were decorated in blue with dolphin birthday streamers, party favors, and helium balloons. Dolphin party bags filled a side table, alongside a large stack of presents. There was lots of food: cheese and pepperoni pizzas, salad, breadsticks, cheese sticks, dipping sauces, and a platter of chocolate cupcakes with blue frosting. Everyone served themselves from the buffet. Melanie watched her parents and friends, eating, talking, laughing, and taking pictures. Her heart bubbled over with happiness.

After dinner, Vivian and Bonnie lit the candles on her cupcakes. The group sang "Happy Birthday" to her. Melanie grinned. When they finished singing, Melanie closed her eyes and wished for the impossible. She wanted to go to camp with her friends.

Melanie gobbled down a cupcake and began to open her presents one by one. She received books, gift cards, and a charm bracelet. Even her sister, Megan, had sent her a gift of a dolphin necklace from Hawaii. She grabbed a prettily decorated box with a frilly bow and curly ribbons. The tag read: From Haley. Melanie unwrapped it and lifted the lid of the white box. It was stuffed with tissue paper. She pulled out a delicate glass figurine. It was a mermaid.

"I would have gotten you a glass dolphin instead if I had known you liked them so much."

"No, this is just perfect. Thank you."

Haley blushed.

Melanie carefully laid the lovely mermaid back into the box. She gave it to her mom and asked her to keep it safe.

"And this is from me." Vivian handed her an envelope.

Melanie opened the card and inside was a photo of Paco. She read what Vivian wrote and looked up. "I don't understand."

"It's your choice. I can buy a bird for you or you can have Paco. But I believe Paco has already decided for you."

"Are you sure you want to give him up?" Melanie's voice squeaked out.

"I know how much he loves you and I think you feel the same."

"Oh, yes. As long as you're fine with it, I want Paco. But are you sure?"

"Yes, I'm sure." Vivian laughed.

"Thank you so much. I'm going to take really good care of him." Tears came to Melanie's eyes as she hugged Vivian.

Next was her parents' gift. Dad gave her a card. Melanie read it and grinned.

"Well, what is it?" Haley asked.

"My parents are going to get me a cage and all the supplies I need to give Paco a good home." She embraced her parents. "Thank you, Mom and Dad." Melanie looked around the room at all her friends gathered there just for her. She was so lucky. "Thank you everyone. This has been the best birthday ever!"

Dad cleared his throat. "Well actually, it's not over yet. There's one more gift." Dad handed her a large manila envelope.

"What's this? I thought I got all my presents from you," Melanie said as she undid the clasp. She pulled out a thick document and unfolded it and read the top line of the form and her eyes widened. "Really?" she squealed.

"Yes, really," Mom said as she and Dad chuckled together.

"What is it, mermaid?" Haley asked.

She turned to her friends. "It's a copy of my registration for junior high camp!"

The girls' yells and screams were deafening, and they encircled her, jumping up and down.

Katie shrieked, "I'm so glad you're finally going to camp!" She squeezed Melanie's shoulder.

Bonnie teased, "I hope you guys aren't this loud when I'm your counselor."

"I don't envy you one bit of this," Dad sympathized with a laugh.

"I'm not planning on getting much sleep."

"Can Katie be in our cabin, even though she doesn't go to our church?" Melanie asked with the other girls pleading, too.

Bonnie said, "I'm sure something can be arranged."

"I can't believe I'm going to camp." She turned toward her parents. "But I thought we couldn't . . . "

Dad raised his hands. "We didn't have anything to do with it, besides filling out the forms for you to go. Bonnie is the one who told us about it."

"Bonnie, you did all this?"

"No, not exactly. Someone found out you wanted to go but couldn't. So, this person, who wants to remain anonymous, started a collection for you. Pastor Brett and I told the youth about it, and they wanted to donate and then it took off from there. Most of the church contributed."

Her friends grinned, but they wouldn't look at her. Melanie's heart radiated with warmth. "This is amazing! Wow! Just wow! This really is the best birthday ever!"

17

SLUMBER PARTY REVELATIONS

After playing a few games, Bonnie and her parents left and Vivian went upstairs to bed. The girls changed into their pj's and decided to watch a movie. Melanie sat in the middle of the couch with Katie and Cindy on either side of her. Rachel stood behind them French braiding Melanie's hair. When the movie ended, they sat at the table and ate more pizza and talked.

Chewing on a piece of pepperoni, Ella asked, "So Melanie, are there any guys you like?"

Melanie bit her lip and Katie rushed in, "I don't think so. She's too busy swimming or reading."

"Well, everyone likes JB. He is just so cute and so sweet." Ella added, "Even Haley likes him."

"Hey!" Haley objected.

"It's true." Rachel defended her friend.

Haley's eyes bulged. "But that was a secret."

Ella guffawed. "How can it be a secret if everybody already knows?"

Haley snarled. "Not everybody."

Cindy quickly glanced at Melanie. "The only thing wrong with JB is his choice of friends."

The girls groaned in agreement.

Rachel raised her eyebrows. "Adam is such a pest, no matter how cute he is. But he's the worst to you Cin, since he likes you."

"Don't say that. He absolutely drives me crazy. But I think you're wrong. He likes Bethany."

Haley snorted. "All the guys like Bethany, since she's so pretty."

"All except JB," Cindy said, "but, I guess he prefers it that way, since he doesn't believe in dating and wears his promise ring."

Melanie was puzzled. What made them think JB didn't believe in dating? And why did he wear a promise ring? She thought promise rings were for people who wanted to get engaged in the future. It didn't make any sense, unless it was some kind of church thing. She would have to ask Katie later if she knew what it meant.

"Bethany has tried everything to get JB's attention. Believe me," Cindy emphasized. "But he doesn't seem to like anyone."

Melanie bit her lip. At the barbecue, JB had said he noticed her at God's Rock. And when he had come over with his mom, she was sure that he might like her. Was she wrong? But why would he like her and not this pretty girl, Bethany?

Katie wrinkled her forehead. "Didn't I meet her last year? She has strawberry-blonde hair, right?"

Rachel nodded and turned to Melanie. "You haven't met her yet, because she lives with her dad in the summer. But enough about JB. He isn't the only guy who is sweet and cute. Trevor is, too."

Cindy made a gagging sound. "My brother! Eww!" She rolled her eyes.

"Do we have to talk about guys all night?" Haley moaned. "Hey, let's open our goody bags."

Each bag on the side table had one of the girl's names on it. Melanie smiled as they oohed and ahhed over the contents. When Katie came back to the table, she held two bags.

"This one is yours, Mel."

"I got one, too?" Sure enough, her name was written in big block letters.

Rachel squealed with pleasure. “There’s nail polish. We should give each other manicures. Melanie’s first.”

Haley lifted her foot. “I’d rather have a pedicure.”

“You can give yourself a pedicure. No one wants to touch your feet.” Ella munched on a chocolate bar.

They laughed except Haley, who stuck out her lip.

Haley burst out, “Kidding.” Then in a sinister voice, she said, “So, what should we do to the person who falls asleep first?” She drummed her fingertips together while raising her eyebrows.

“We will think about that later,” Rachel said brushing her off. She motioned to the bottles of nail polish lined up on the table. “So, which color do you want, Melanie?”

“Actually, if everyone doesn’t mind, I would love it if I could use all the colors so I can have a color from each of my friends.”

As Rachel painted her nails, Melanie questioned, “Did you guys know about the camp collection for me?” She glanced at them, but again they had trouble keeping eye contact with her. “Come on, someone say something.”

Haley was first to speak. “Of course, we knew about it. We all wanted you to go.”

"I wish we'd thought of it though," Cindy said.

"So, you guys don't know whose idea it was?"

They shook their heads.

After they finished their nails, the girls headed back to the great room and sat on their sleeping bags, except for Haley. She cleaned up after them and said in a sing-song voice, "Look at me. I'm pitching in."

The girls burst out laughing. All except for Melanie. "What's so funny?"

It took them a few minutes to stop laughing. Katie was even wiping her eyes. When they calmed down, Katie told her about the improv group, which had performed skits for the campers.

"Their 'Pitching In' skit is hilarious." Katie turned to the other girls. "We should show Melanie all of their videos."

"Yeah, we can watch them on my phone." Ella volunteered.

They played the goof-ball skits over and over. Melanie's sides ached from laughter at their crazy stunts.

"Oh, I hope they'll be there this year, too. I feel like I missed so much."

"Hey!" Katie said. "It's your own fault. I begged you to go last year. I even begged you to go this year. And I finally got my way. Ha!"

There was a loud snore and the girls turned around. Haley was out.

Ella drummed her fingertips together and imitated Haley perfectly. "Oh, what should we do to Haley since she fell asleep first?"

They giggled.

18

KATIE'S VISIT

On Saturday, Melanie and Katie rested on a log, leaning their backs against a large boulder. The meandering creek splashed a peaceful tune and the sweet scent of redwood trees surrounded them. Afternoon sunlight draped them in warmth.

Katie mused, "If I close my eyes, I'd think I was in my favorite spot at camp. Of course, mine is more sheltered by the trees."

"Maybe you can show it to me when we go. Why do you like it so much?"

"For some reason, it's there that I feel closest to God." She sighed. "That was a great party. I hope Haley appreciates that you kept everyone from pulling any pranks on her."

Melanie chuckled. "It was fun to plan what to do but carrying it out on someone who's my friend just didn't seem right."

"I wouldn't be surprised if they try something at camp, especially since Haley is such a heavy sleeper." Katie shaded her eyes with her hand. "It's getting too hot out here. Let's go inside."

They lounged across from each other in the window seat of Melanie's bedroom, soaking in the peacefulness. Melanie was tired, but she hoped to spend as much time with Katie as possible.

"I still can't believe your room is so clean."

"I promised my mom I'd clean it if you stayed with us for my birthday."

"Wow, I feel so special." Katie raised her eyebrows and smiled. "So, tell me, how long is it going to stay this way?"

Melanie threw a pillow at her.

"I guess that means not long if you're already making a mess."

She picked up another pillow and pretended like she was going to toss it at Katie. "If you can believe it, I've actually missed your teasing." Melanie hesitated. "I'm not sure if I want to tell you this or not, since I don't want to hear you say I told you so."

Katie laughed. "I'm pretty sure I already know what you're going to say. You like living here, don't you?"

She nodded. "Actually, I can hardly believe it myself, but yes."

"I knew it." Katie clapped her hands.

"I didn't want you to say I told you so."

"I didn't." Katie playfully stuck her tongue out.

Melanie bit her lip, afraid of hurting Katie's feelings with what she wanted to ask. "Are . . . you upset with me for going to church?"

"Of course not. Don't be silly."

"But I didn't go to your church."

"Oh, I see what you mean. Melanie, I would've loved if you'd gone to my church, but what I really want is for you to know God."

Melanie was puzzled. "My mom said something like that, too, but I don't understand what it means."

Katie explained. "I don't understand everything about God either, but I know He loves you. And when you love someone, you want what's best for them. God wants to show you His love. He wants you to spend time with Him and get to know Him. Mel, you're my best friend and I really miss you. But the things I've been praying about for you for so long have finally been coming true."

Melanie's eyebrows lowered. "Like, what kind of things did you pray for me?"

She paused and gave a lopsided grin. "I've been praying you would make some Christian friends, and that you'd go to church."

"I've prayed, too. Well, not about that, but I did pray."

"You have? What did you pray about?"

"I prayed that God would show me that He loved and cared for me and that He would give me peace. At the time I prayed, He did give me peace. And now I know He does love and care for me and my family. He took care of Mom when she got hurt and then He gave me a party and because the church cared, too, I'm going to camp."

Katie reached over and hugged her. "I'm so happy. We should thank God for what He has done."

Melanie gulped. "Okay."

They folded their legs and scooted closer together facing each other. Melanie grabbed Katie's hand and Katie took her other hand. They bowed their heads and closed their eyes.

"Dear God, thank you for my friend, Melanie." Katie squeezed her hands. "Also thank you that Melanie is able to go to camp. Help Melanie understand what a relationship with You is like and what it means. Thank you, too, for answering my prayers about Melanie. In Jesus' name."

Melanie was a little nervous, since this was her first time praying out loud. "Dear God, thank you for my surprise party and for being able to go to camp, and thank you for my new friends, and an old one, too. Amen."

Katie squeezed her hand again before she let go. "All right, are you going to tell me more about this JB or what?" She raised her eyebrows and smiled. "I can tell you like him."

Melanie playfully slapped her on the arm and released a grin she could no longer hold back. "Maybe." She told Katie about meeting him and how he came over to the house and they talked. "I really like him. I know the girls said he doesn't like anyone, but I have a feeling he likes me, too." She shook her head. "But I'm confused about him having a promise ring. Do you know what it means?"

Katie attempted to explain. "I think so. He goes to your church, right?

Melanie nodded.

"Then I believe it's a promise to God."

"But what did he promise to God?"

"From what the girls said last night, he isn't going to be dating, but it could mean even more. Most promise rings symbolize that the person is saving themselves until they get married. I know you're not going to like this idea, but if you want to know the specifics about JB's promise, you'll have to ask him."

"Well, that isn't going to happen."

"From what you told me and from what the girls said, he seems like a great guy."

"We should see him at church on Sunday."

"Maybe you could introduce me," Katie teased.

Her comment brought on a fit of laughter for them both.

19

HOMECOMING

Melanie was trying to finish setting up Paco's new cage, but she was distracted. Deep inside, something was bothering her. Why did she feel this way? She had gotten practically everything she had asked for and more—a wonderful birthday party, the chance to go to camp, and a bird of her very own. She frowned.

It was because she missed Dad. She knew she should be grateful to God for answering her prayers over the last few weeks. But if He could just answer one more, she might believe God wanted to draw her . . . what had Pastor Brett said? "Draw her closer to knowing Him."

Melanie didn't know what to do. She slumped down next to Mom on the couch.

"Why didn't Dad come up this weekend? He promised he would."

"I don't know. I'm sure he has a good reason." Mom stroked Melanie's arm. "Mel, I'm really proud of you. You've grown up so much this summer. I think this move has been good for you."

Melanie nodded. "I guess it has. I have new friends, new interests, and I've changed the way I feel about God. I don't know when my feelings changed toward Him, but I know He cares about me. He cares about us. And I'm beginning to see the good things that He has done for our family." She paused, then continued, "I even like going to church. The people there treat us as though we're family."

Mom nodded. "I love that about it, too."

"Mom, I hope that we don't have to move back. I would miss Vivian and my new friends. I didn't realize I would like it here so much."

"You could pray about it," Mom suggested.

Melanie bit her lip. "Actually, I have prayed."

"I'm glad to hear that, but you can ask God for things more than once. Would you like to pray together?"

She nodded and closed her eyes. "God, I don't understand. Why does Dad have to be away from us?

I miss him so much." She sighed. "I even miss Megan. Would you please bring them home to stay?"

Mom prayed, too, and when they said amen, they heard a car pull up in the driveway. Melanie got up to see who it was. Whoever these people were, they were a bit early to be dropping off dinner. The door opened before she could reach it. How rude. Who would do such a thing? Melanie prepared to glare at the intruder.

"Hey, Squirt."

"Megan?" Melanie gasped. "What are you doing here?"

"We live here now, remember?" Megan's skin was a golden-tan and her blonde hair had lightened even more.

"But you're supposed to be in Hawaii. What happened?"

"We were having fun, but when I heard about Mom getting hurt, and . . . well don't get too excited." She huffed. "I missed you guys."

Melanie hugged her. At first, Megan just patted her, and then she laughed and hugged back. "I guess this means you missed me, too."

"Yes, I did," Melanie confessed.

While Megan was busy hugging Mom, Melanie slipped outside to see Dad. He was pulling out multiple suitcases and adding them to a pile of boxes which blocked the driveway.

"Wow, how much did Megan bring back?"

Dad raised his eyebrows and smiled. "It isn't all Megan's."

"Oh." She bit her lip. "Does this mean . . . ?"

"It means that we're all living here together."

Melanie squealed and threw her arms around him. He chuckled and kissed the top of her head. She looked up at him. "But what about your job?"

"I quit. I missed my family too much. Funny thing is that once I decided to quit, I was offered a job here by one of the men I met at the Fourth of July barbecue." He grinned. "Are you glad?"

Melanie beamed. "More than you know."

"Now, let's get inside and tell your mom."

When they came in, Mom had already heard the news.

"Is it really true, Jack?"

Dad nodded. "This is our home."

Melanie looked at Mom. "Did you know about this?"

Mom shook her head.

"Know about what, Squirt? That we were coming? Nope. Dad and I wanted to surprise you and I guess we did. Hey, you're wearing the necklace I gave you for your birthday."

Thumbing the dolphin pendant, Melanie said, "I love it."

"So, I need to know the scoop. Are there any cute boys around here? Oh, wait a minute. You don't like boys yet, do you?"

A blush heated Melanie's cheeks.

"You do! You have to tell me."

Dad huffed. "I don't think I want to hear about this." He playfully put his hands over his ears. "I guess this happens when you have girls, but I was hoping I had a few more years left with Melanie. I was hoping your swimming would keep you preoccupied. I guess my mermaid has to grow up sometime but I didn't think it would be this soon." He laughed. "Now that I'm home—maybe I can scare them away."

Megan exhaled. "Enough already, Dad." She pulled her suitcase toward their room. "You should see all the stuff I brought back with me. I thought we could decorate our room with a tropical theme. It would go well with your collection of dolphins."

Melanie's eyes grew in alarm. "Well, about our room . . . "

Megan groaned, returning to her bossy self. "I'll help you clean it, but just this once. You better keep it clean from now on."

"I'll try." Melanie started to follow her with an enormous grin on her face.

It really worked. She had prayed they would come home, and they did. Melanie mumbled softly, "Thank you, God."

"What did you say, Mel?" Dad asked.

"Nevermind." She smiled even bigger and glanced at Mom, who nodded and winked.

They were together and life was back to normal. Well, not exactly, but a new kind of normal. And camp was just around the corner. God did care about her and love her and had made things good. What else might He have in store for her? She couldn't wait to find out.

Discussion Questions

Chapter 1

1. Have you ever accidentally overheard a conversation that you shouldn't have?
2. Do you have a sport you compete in and enjoy?
3. Is winning important? Or is doing your best what's more important?
4. Sometimes parents make decisions we don't understand. How would God want us to act in those kind of situations?

Chapter 2

1. Do your parents have a nickname for you?
2. Should Melanie have confessed to her parents about the truth of why she hadn't been sleeping?

3. Should Megan have reacted the way she did when her parents announced they were moving?
4. How would you feel if you and your family had to move unexpectedly?
5. Has any of your friends misunderstood what you meant?
6. Do you think God wants us unhappy? Why or why not?

Chapter 3

1. Does your family have a special place where you all spend time together?
2. Have you ever seen an aviary? If so, what did you like about it?
3. Is it okay for parents to argue?
4. Should Melanie's dad provide for the family or keep his promise?

Chapter 4

1. When you see/meet a new person are you friendly with them?
2. Are you talkative like Cindy or are you shy like Melanie or somewhere in between?

3. Do you attend a church youth group? If so, does it have a name?
4. Do you have a pet? How do you take care of your pet?
5. Do you blame God for your problems?

Chapter 5

1. Do you get nervous when you do something new or meet new people?
2. Do you enjoy singing worship songs?
3. Do you memorize verses? Romans 8:28 is a good verse to have memorized.
4. Will life be perfect after you became a Christian?
5. Has God used your circumstances to draw you closer to Him? Think about an example.

Chapter 6

1. Is it God's fault when life doesn't go the way we think it should?
2. What are things you are thankful for?
3. Has someone ever broken a promise to you? How did it make you feel?
4. Do you like to read? Do you have a friend you like to discuss books with?

Chapter 7

1. Do you have your own Bible?
2. Have you ever said something that later you regretted like when Melanie mentions that Pastor Brett is goofy to Bonnie?
3. Have you ever gone to summer camp?

Chapter 8

1. Have you ever been part of a team? What was it?
2. Have you ever had to make a hard decision?
3. Do you have a friend you can't be around all the time because of long distance?

Chapter 9

1. Have you been disappointed when you cannot do something all of your friends are doing?
2. Should Melanie participate in the fundraiser?
3. Melanie is getting what she wants, but she doesn't want it anymore. Have you ever changed your mind about something?
4. Do you ever have to make tough choices?

Chapter 10

1. Have you ever waited for your friends to come and was disappointed that they didn't show up?
2. Have you ever been picked on?
3. Do you ask God to help you when you're upset?
4. If someone is hurting, how can you help them?

Chapter 11

1. When you have problems, do you ask God to help you?
2. When bad things happen to us, should you tell your parents?
3. What did Melanie's mom mean when she asked Jesus to forgive her sins and become Lord of her life?
4. Have you prayed about something and felt God's peace?

Chapter 12

1. Have you ever worked on a surprise for someone like Melanie and her mom are doing to make an office for Melanie's dad?
2. What do you do in the face of an emergency?

3. Has someone you care about been hurt in an accident? Were you able to help them?

Chapter 13

1. Has someone been there for you when something bad happened?
2. Have you ever helped someone in need?
3. Things happen in our life that seem bad, but God can bring something good from it. Have you seen God bring something good from a bad situation?
4. Are you willing to allow God to work in your life to bring out something good?

Chapter 14

1. How do you think it made Melanie's family feel when the church people reached out to them?
2. Have you ever given something up in order to help someone you love? This is called sacrificial love.

Chapter 15

1. Have you or your family reached out to someone in need?

2. How can you be helpful to others who may need a helping hand?
3. Do you visit others who are sick or lonely?
4. Have you ever felt brave?

Chapter 16

1. Is is hard for you to keep a secret like Katie did?
2. Melanie received some thoughtful gifts, have you given a special heartfelt gift to someone?
3. Have you ever tried to raise money for a cause in order to help someone you know? How about raising money to help a stranger? (See donation page)

Chapter 17

1. What do you talk about with your friends?
2. Do you share secrets with your friends?
3. Do you help clean up when you are at a friend's house?

Chapter 18

1. Do you care about your friends feelings?
2. Do you want your friends to know about God? Do you know about God?

3. Do you pray for your friends? Do you want what is best for them—to know God and His love?
4. Do you thank God when He does something for you?
5. Do you wear a promise ring? Do you know anyone who wears a promise ring?
6. Have you made any promises to God? What are they?

Chapter 19

1. What has God done in your life to draw you closer to Him?
2. Do you feel that God cares about you? What are ways that He has shown you His love?
3. Do you pray with your parents?
4. God doesn't always answer our prayers right away but sometimes He does. How has God answered your prayers?
5. In Melanie's fictional world everything turns out all right. Real life isn't like that. But we can use Romans 8:28 to give us hope that God will work good into our circumstances. What things in your life

were bad which God brought about good to come from it?

6. God cares about you and loves you. What might He have in store for your future?

Acknowledgments

So many people have encouraged, supported, and helped me on my writing journey, especially with this book. I am eternally grateful to them, and with my heart I give thanks. I include them in this list, and if I have forgotten anyone, please forgive me.

- My amazing Heavenly Father who through my trials and struggles gave me beautiful gifts which I can never repay but I will always be exceedingly thankful for
- My husband, Matt, who loves me and supports all of my crazy dreams
- My family and adoptive family, Poppy, Mommy, Sissy, Trevor, Tyler Jordan, Jared, Geri, Carlos, Mom and Dad Rempel, Jesse, Paula, Blake, Bailey, Lewis, and Tommy—thank you for your love and support
- My extended family who are too numerous to count
- My critique partners over the years, Nancy, Donna, Ellen, John, Amy, Jan, and Carl, God has used you to help with the calling on my life

- My good friends, Bonnie and Rachel, I enjoyed naming characters after you to show you how much your love and friendship has meant to me over the years.
- My newest friend, Jakki, your friendship and help has been a gift to me
- Sarah and Susan, for your encouragement and endorsements
- Tim Carlisle, I was never your student but you encouraged my writing dreams
- My editors, Lindsay A. Franklin and Daphne Self, thank you for teaching me more about writing and also for hearing my writer's voice
- Ambassador International, Sam, Anna, and Hannah, thank you for believing in me and this book. My hope is that we touch many young hearts to know our God.
- My church families, Good News Family Fellowship and Hillside Alliance Church
- Oregon Christian Writers, for your ministry to us writers
- Alliance Redwoods Conference Grounds and Staff, for providing a place to reconnect to God and helping others find Him
- Christian musicians, also too numerous to count, thank you for your influence in my life and drawing me closer to my Savior

Donate

The NorCal Girls series was inspired by my family trips to camp. We spent many wonderful summers at Alliance Redwood Conference Grounds. A portion of the proceeds from this series will be donated to ARCG toward the general fund and the scholarship fund so other kids can go to camp. You can donate, too, at www.allianceredwoods.com/give.

For more information about

J.D. Rempel
and
Melanie on the Move
please connect:

www.jdrempel.com
www.facebook.com/jdrempel
@jdrempelwriter
www.instagram.com/j.d.rempel

For more information about
AMBASSADOR INTERNATIONAL
please connect:

www.ambassador-international.com
@AmbassadorIntl
www.facebook.com/AmbassadorIntl

If you enjoyed this book, please consider leaving us a review on Amazon, Goodreads, or our website.

More from Ambassador International

Daisy's search for freedom leads her deep into the woods. Along the way she is joined by Simon, a four-year-old boy and his pet kitten. Pursued by dogs, uncertainty, and a slave tracker determined to capture them by any means necessary, Daisy starts to wonder if she will ever be safe again. Does Jesus care about runaway slaves lost in the woods? Book one in The Searchers series.

Daisy's Search for Freedom
by Bertha Schwartz

Miriam is asked to do the impossible: serve the wife of Naaman, commander of the Syrian army. Clinging to treasured memories of home and faith, Miriam faces captivity with worry and bitterness. Little does she know the Heart Changer is wooing and preparing her for a greater mission far beyond what she could imagine.

The Heart Changer
Jarm Del Boccio

An inspiring story of a cranky crow, a sick little girl, a kind squirrel, and Monday's struggle to deal with his own crackability.

The Cracking of Monday Egg
by B.T. Higgins

Made in the USA
San Bernardino, CA
22 May 2020

72147835R00086